Aeronautics

Other books in the Careers for the Twenty-First Century series:

Law Enforcement
Medicine
The News Media

Careers
for the
Twenty-First
Century

Aeronautics

By Christina M. Girod

LUCENT BOOKS
SAN DIEGO, CALIFORNIA

THOMSON

─────★───── ™

GALE

Detroit • New York • San Diego • San Francisco
Boston • New Haven, Conn. • Waterville, Maine
London • Munich

Library of Congress Cataloging-in-Publication Data

Girod, Christina M.
  Aeronautics / by Christina M. Girod
    p.   cm. — (Careers in the 21st century)
  Includes bibliographical references and index.
  Summary: Covers the various positions available in the field of aeronautics, discussing
  qualifications, training, job opportunities, and technological advances in airplanes and
  space craft.
  ISBN 1-56006-894-9 (hardback: alk. paper)
    1. Aeronautics—Vocational guidance—Juvenile literature. [1. Aeronautics—
  Vocational guidance. 2. Vocational guidance.] I. Title.   II. Careers in the 21st
  century (San Diego, Calif.)
  TL561.G57 2002
  629.13'0023—dc21   53292

2002005792

Contents

Foreword

Young people in the twenty-first century are faced with a dizzying array of possibilities for careers as they become adults. However, the advances of technology and a world economy in which events in one nation increasingly affect events in other nations have made the job market extremely competitive. Young people entering the job market today must possess a combination of technological knowledge and an understanding of the cultural and socioeconomic factors that affect the working world. Don Tapscott, internationally known author and consultant on the effects of technology in business, government, and society, supports this idea, saying, "Yes, this country needs more technology graduates, as they fuel the digital economy. But . . . we have an equally strong need for those with a broader [humanities] background who can work in tandem with technical specialists, helping create and manage the [workplace] environment." To succeed in this job market young people today must enter it with a certain amount of specialized knowledge, preparation, and practical experience. In addition, they must possess the drive to update their job skills continually to match rapidly occurring technological, economic, and social changes.

Young people entering the twenty-first-century job market must carefully research and plan the education and training they will need to work in their chosen career. High school graduates can no longer go straight into a job where they can hope to advance to positions of higher pay, better working conditions, and increased responsibility without first entering a training program, trade school, or college. For example, aircraft mechanics must attend schools that offer Federal Aviation Administration–accredited programs. These programs offer a broad-based curriculum that requires students to demonstrate an understanding of the basic principles of flight, aircraft function, and electronics. Students must also master computer technology used for diagnosing problems and show that they can apply what they learn toward routine maintenance and any number of needed repairs. With further education, an aircraft mechanic can gain increasingly specialized licenses that place him or her in the job market for positions of higher pay and greater responsibility.

In addition to technology skills, young people must understand how to communicate and work effectively with colleagues or clients from diverse backgrounds. James Billington, librarian of Congress, ascertains that "we do not have a global village, but rather a globe on which there are a whole lot of new villages . . . each trying to get its own place in the world, and anybody who's going to deal with this world is going to have to relate better to more of it." For example, flight attendants are increasingly being expected to know one or more foreign languages in order for them to better serve the needs of international passengers. Electrical engineers collaborating with a sister company in Russia on a project must be aware of cultural differences that could affect communication between the project members and, ultimately, the success of the project.

The Lucent Books Careers for the Twenty-First Century series discusses how these ideas come into play in such competitive career fields as aeronautics, biotechnology, computer technology, engineering, education, law enforcement, and medicine. Each title in the series discusses from five to seven different careers available in the respective field. The series provides a comprehensive view of what it's like to work in a particular job and what it takes to succeed in it. Each chapter encompasses a career's most recent trends in education and training, job responsibilities, the work environment and conditions, special challenges, earnings, and opportunities for advancement. Primary and secondary source quotes enliven the text. Sidebars expand on issues related to each career, including topics such as gender issues in the workplace, personal stories that demonstrate exceptional on the job experiences, and the latest technology and its potential for use in a particular career. Every volume includes an Organizations to Contact list as well as annotated bibliographies. Books in this series provide readers with pertinent information for deciding on a career, and a launching point for further research.

Aeronautics: A Mainstay of Modern Life

Throughout the centuries humankind has been fascinated with flight. People longed to take to the skies, free of physical limitations. It took many years and many mistakes until at last people discovered the secrets of sustained flight, beginning with the Wright brothers at Kitty Hawk, North Carolina, in 1903.

In the nearly one hundred years since the Wright brothers' first flight, aircraft have become complex technological birds of steel, in many shapes and sizes, and serving a variety of purposes. The military uses aircraft for attacking enemies, transporting supplies, spying, and medical relief. Commercial aircraft are used to transport packages, mail, and even large items such as vehicles across oceans and continents. Passenger airliners move people, traveling for business or pleasure, from state to state or country to country in a matter of hours.

Because flying has become a mainstay of modern life, the business of flying aircraft has become an integral part of the world. This business is called aeronautics, which is defined as the operation of aircraft. The people who work in aeronautics are the ones who make flying possible. The people who fly planes, who build them, who repair them, who direct them, who make them both safe and comfortable enable planes to take to the skies, getting passengers and cargo to their destinations safely and quickly.

Aeronautics has always held a kind of magic for the people who work in the field. Although their jobs are often tough and sometimes dangerous, most of them carry on a love affair with their chosen profession. People in aeronautics work in many different capacities, each of which is an important part of the business of flying. The job of pilot is perhaps the most popular with the public; pilots are the ones who fly those amazing birds of steel. Flight attendants are the most visible to the public, as they are the ones who take care of passengers' needs and help during emergencies. Aircraft mechanics inspect and repair planes, working quickly but in accordance with high safety standards, to keep planes operating on time. A natural outgrowth of aeronautics has been the development of aerospace, which deals with the earth's atmosphere and the space beyond it. Many people who work in aeronautics go on to become astronauts, those who travel in aerospace in a spacecraft. Astronauts spend a great deal of time flying in jets while training for missions in space. Some astronauts are pilots and operate the space shuttle, a type of spacecraft.

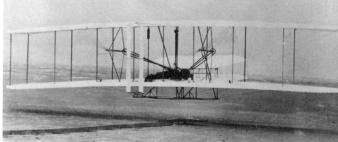

The Wright brothers (below) completed the first sustained flight at Kitty Hawk, North Carolina, in 1903.

Although the training and education needed for each type of job differ widely, almost all people who work in the field of aeronautics enjoy certain benefits that no other field can offer. Typically, employees of airlines are eligible for free or reduced airfare for themselves and their immediate families. Another attractive benefit available to most airline employees is a retirement plan that includes a pension plus participation in a stock and bond plan, in an age when most companies are paring down their retirement benefits. In addition, airline employees receive life and health insurance benefits comparable to those offered in other professions.

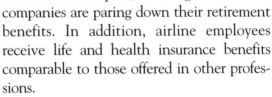

NASA's space shuttle Endeavor *carries astronauts into space.*

As the twenty-first century begins, passenger and cargo traffic continue to rise. During the next decade projected increases in population, income, and business will swell the job market in aeronautics by 18 percent. More planes in the air will require more pilots to fly them, more mechanics to service them, and more flight attendants to serve passengers. Increased air traffic will mean more controllers will be needed to manage the flow in and out of airports. In addition, growing technological advances and scientific research will render space travel for commercial and scientific reasons more efficient and attractive.

Regardless of the technological advances or the quickening pace of work, people who work in aeronautics will continue to love their jobs. What all of them have in common is a fascination with flight and a love of adventure. People in aeronautics thrive on challenges and the daily changes they encounter at work. Perhaps Tom Zaccheo, an air traffic controller, sums up what those in the field of aeronautics feel about their work: "This whole job is an endurance test, from the first day until you retire. And you know who holds the whole thing together? We do. We don't do it for the FAA [Federal Aviation Administration], and we don't do it for the airlines. We do it for ourselves. We just keep pumping tin."[1]

Chapter 1

Pilots

A pilot is a highly trained professional who flies airplanes and helicopters. Pilots fly a variety of aircraft to accomplish many different tasks, from transporting passengers to tracking criminals to dusting farmland crops with pesticides. Overall, however, pilots are in their profession because they love to fly. Pilot Richard Bach writes about the spirit of the pilot:

> Why would anyone, you ask . . . become an airplane pilot? At the question . . . the pilots stare at you for not knowing the clearly obvious.
>
> "Why, flying saves time, that's why," says the business pilot, at last.

Airplane pilots navigate a 747 jet.

"Because it's fun, and no other reason matters," says the sport pilot.

"Dummies!" says the professional pilot. "Everybody knows that this is the best way in the world to make a living!"

"Well, we defied gravity one more time." Reflected in that common after-flight saying is a hint of the tie that binds airmen together, each in his own world. Airborne, the airman is matching himself against whatever the sky has to offer. The sky and the airplane combine in a challenge, and the airman . . . has decided to accept that challenge.[2]

Becoming a Pilot

Despite the exhilaration pilots feel for their jobs, it takes years of hard work to get to the apex of their careers. There are basically two ways for pilots to start their careers: in the military or as students.

About half of all commercial pilots begin their careers in the military by joining the air force, the navy, the marine corps, or the coast guard. There are benefits as well as drawbacks to receiving pilot training in the military. The benefits include getting paid to train on some of the most sophisticated aircraft available, including fighters, bombers, and transport vehicles. These can be either planes or helicopters. In exchange, a person must commit to ten years of service in the armed forces. This means years of living a military life of following orders, risking bodily harm, and using dangerous weapons. In addition, military pilots must complete some college coursework—usually in engineering and mathematics—and must maintain good health.

The military is not the ideal training place for everyone, however, and many pilots are trained at FAA-certified flight schools or in colleges or universities that offer degrees in aviation along with flight training. After completing the program of study; passing a written examination on flight principles, safety, navigation, and regulations; and logging at least 250 hours of airtime, civilian pilots must pass a check-ride, which pilot Joel Freeman describes as "something like the driving test we take to get our driver's licenses. A Federal Aviation Administration (FAA) examiner asks you to plan a flight, quizzes you on aviation matters and then accompanies you on a flight."[3] If the check-ride goes well the examiner will issue a commercial pilot's license.

A fighter pilot steers a plane. Nearly half of all commercial pilots begin their careers in the military.

The commercial pilot's license, however, is only a basic license, and much more training is needed to gain the more advanced licenses required to get a job as a pilot. To work for an airline, a pilot must also have an instrument rating from the FAA, which certifies that the pilot is proficient in flying aircraft "blind," meaning by instruments alone. To qualify for an instrument rating a pilot must have logged 105 hours of airtime, including forty hours of flying by instruments alone. In addition, the pilot must demonstrate proficiency in flying by instruments to an examiner and must pass a written test on instrument flying.

After a commercial pilot's license, the next advanced license is an airline transport certificate, which certifies that a pilot has at least fifteen hundred hours of airtime, experience with both night and instrument flying, and an advanced rating, such as certification to fly different types of aircraft or planes with several engines. This is the license that will allow a pilot to eventually work as a captain in command of the jumbo jets for major airlines.

Where Pilots Work

However, it is very difficult for a pilot to get a job with a major airline early in his or her career. Most airlines will hire only pilots with the most advanced training and thousands of flight hours logged. As a result, many pilots work in a variety of jobs other than as airline pilots. About 16 percent of pilots work for other businesses or organizations. Some work for courier lines, such as Federal Express; for tourist companies that offer sightseeing by helicopter or by small plane; or for corporations that need pilots to fly executives, clients, or cargo on their planes. A small number also work for the FAA as administrators or teach at FAA-certified flight schools.

Other pilots work for farms or for government agencies that deal with agriculture. These pilots are responsible for flying over large areas of land and spreading seeds, fertilizer, or pesticides. Many large-scale farmers need pilots to help them plant crop seeds or dust growing crops with toxic chemicals to kill pests that harm the crops. Federal agencies such as the National Forest Service need pilots to help in reseeding areas where forests have been heavily logged, burned, or otherwise damaged.

Besides agricultural piloting jobs, pilots also work in public service jobs. Fire-fighting pilots fly helicopters over fires and spray water and chemicals on the burning areas to squelch the flames. They may fight wildfires over a huge expanse of land or they may douse fires in buildings or other structures. Some pilots work for law enforcement agencies and fly helicopters to help track fleeing or escaped criminals or suspects. Pilots may work for local television news companies, flying reporters over major freeways and streets in urban areas, or over accidents, so that traffic conditions may be reported accurately. Search-and-rescue pilots are like flying ambulance drivers. They often fly to remote areas where someone has been hurt and use special equipment to bring the injured person to safety. Then a paramedic provides emergency medical care while the pilot flies the injured person to the nearest hospital.

Although public service piloting jobs can be perilous, the job of a test pilot is considered one of the most dangerous but exciting jobs in the field of aeronautics. Most test pilots are experienced military pilots who make their living flying experimental aircraft. They check new models and types to ensure they work at optimum safety and efficiency standards.

Types of Airplanes

When most people think of airplanes, they think of long, sleek jumbo jets cruising in and out of airports. However, there are several other types of airplanes that are used in many different ways.

Cargo or transport airplanes have large spaces within them for carrying things that are too big or too heavy for other types of planes to carry. These planes, such as the Boeing 757 freighter and the Airbus Guppy, can carry trucks, large numbers of packages, construction equipment, or even smaller aircraft.

Military airplanes are used for various activities and can be identified by a letter in their names. Military cargo/transport airplanes, such as the C7, are capable of carrying armies, supplies, and equipment. Spy planes are used to fly into hostile areas to take photographs or observe the enemy. Fighter planes, such as the F-16, use different types of advanced technology to attack the enemy. Some fighters can fly faster than the speed of sound while others have stealth ability, meaning they can escape radar detection and thus become invisible to enemy radar screens.

Experimental airplanes are those that are newly designed by engineers and may use a new concept or advanced technology in their design. Experimental planes, such as the X-36, are one or two of a kind, and are flown by test pilots, who rate their performance.

Passenger airplanes can be small, carrying only about twelve people, or large jumbo jets, such as the Boeing 757, that can carry about five hundred people. Most passenger jetliners can travel up to six hundred miles per hour, but the unique Concorde can go twice the speed of sound—fourteen hundred miles per hour.

Although some pilots stay with smaller lines or in public service jobs, by far the majority—84 percent—move on to work for the major airlines. The visibility of the major airlines has been attributed to the public's glamorization of the job of an airline pilot, as Freeman explains:

A person who takes a multimilliondollar machine, casually flies it off the ground and then safely returns it, fascinates people. They wonder what it's like to be responsible for hundreds of lives or goods worth millions. When passengers peek inside a cockpit, they are amazed. They stare at the multitude of dials and ask incredulously, "Do you really know what they all do?"[4]

Preflight Duties and Planning

The answer is yes, airline pilots do know what all those dials do. They must know all that and much more because the most important responsibility any pilot has is for the safety of the crew, passengers, and cargo in an aircraft. It is also the pilot's job to make a flight as energy and time efficient as possible. This saves airlines fuel costs and moves passengers and cargo to their destinations quickly.

A pilot can ensure a safe and efficient flight by making proper planning decisions. The preflight planning used to be exclusively the job of the pilot, but today computers and a large support staff make many of these decisions in the major airlines. Nevertheless, before a flight the pilot must choose a route, an altitude, and a speed, taking into account current weather conditions and the forecast all along the chosen route. Obviously the pilot will choose the shortest route possible with the best weather conditions. The altitude chosen will also depend on the weather conditions and how fast the pilot wants to fly. An airline captain who uses the pseudonym Captain X reveals what the preflight planning is like for him:

The computations involved are incredibly complicated. They'll [computers and support staff] have taken into account all my fuel-burns and wind conditions; they have me vectoring around, or going higher, or descending, and it will be figured with a finesse I couldn't possibly have duplicated. When I first started flying all this stuff was the pilot's job. You figured it yourself. . . . Whatever you came up with . . . well, that's what you were stuck with. You couldn't have possibly figured it out down to the last fraction of a unit of wind velocity. Today it's done for you. It's been computed by your support personnel. There are hundreds of people behind each and every airplane flight. There'll be a release form attached that holds the pilot responsible, but it's not just one [person], it's a whole corporation up there.[5]

In addition to planning, pilots must check all the aircraft systems to make sure they are working properly before taking off. The pilot checks to make sure that there is ample fuel for the flight, that the engines and landing gear are functioning, and that the hydraulics, pressurizing, air conditioning, and other systems are operating. If the pilot discovers that there is a glitch in a system or that something is not functioning properly, a mechanic is called in to diagnose and correct the problem.

Once the preflight inspection has been completed and it has been determined the aircraft is ready for flight, then the pilot double checks the weather forecast for the proposed route and altitude and then files an instrument flight plan with air traffic control at the airport from which the plane will be departing.

The purpose of the instrument flight plan is to provide air traffic control with the whereabouts of the plane when there is poor visibility and the pilot must control the plane using instruments on the control panel. By knowing what altitude, route, and speed a pilot plans to fly while instrument flying, air traffic control can ensure that planes flying near each other in poor weather conditions are not on a collision course.

This pilot gives a thumbs-up after completing an aircraft inspection.

Flying by instruments has become easier because the control instruments of most modern aircraft are computerized. This means that the computer keeps the plane steady on its route, at the set altitude and speed. Computerized instrument flight systems can also guide a pilot to a landing strip or runway if the pilot cannot see where the plane is going. For example, the electronic instrument landing system (ILS) uses a radio and a display of horizontal and vertical lines that simulate the runway at the destination airport. Using the grid made by the lines on the display, a pilot can line the plane up on the center of the runway by lining it up on the center of the grid. Nevertheless, sometimes instrument flying can be precarious, as this helicopter traffic reporter reveals:

On climb-out [takeoff] we were solid IFR [instrument flight rules] in a snow shower at 800 feet. I put my head down and climbed another thousand feet, breaking out on top of the scattered clouds to review the situation. Behind, the runway lights were visible, twinkling against the blackness of the surrounding hills. To turn back would entail the risk of encountering IFR conditions again.[6]

Takeoffs and Landings

Despite the risks associated with flying in poor weather, accidents are actually most likely to occur during takeoff or landing. This is partly because these procedures are guided more by people rather than by computers, thereby increasing the risk of human error, and because both involve a complicated mix of precision and cooperation between the piloting crew and air traffic control. During either procedure there is a slight chance of collision with other planes on the runways or of getting caught in wind shear, which is a sudden change in the speed and direction of wind over a very short distance.

Supersonic airliner Concorde during takeoff. Most airplane accidents take place during takeoff or landing.

How an Airplane Flies

Whenever a huge airplane, which can weigh as much as five hundred thousand pounds, takes off, people gaze at the ascending technological wonder with a sense of amazement. How does something so large and so heavy fly in the air?

The answer to how airplanes fly is actually quite simple. When a plane accelerates as it moves down the runway, the air moves under and over the wings, which are shaped to make the air act a certain way. An airplane wing is flat on the bottom and curved on the top, causing the air under it to move slower than the air going over the top of the wing. This is where the Bernoulli effect, which states that slow-moving air causes high pressure and fast-moving air causes low pressure, takes place. Since the air on top moves faster, the air pressure there is low; meanwhile, the slower-moving air underneath the wing causes higher pressure. It is the higher pressure underneath that pushes the wings up, creating a force called lift. As long as the airplane moves at a certain speed the lift will remain, keeping the airplane soaring through the sky.

Wind shear can cause a pilot to lose control of the plane. Even more frightening is a phenomenon called a microburst, which is a sudden downdraft that causes extremely violent wind shear at a low altitude. Although a microburst may last only a minute, it can force a plane approaching a landing strip to suddenly nose-dive into the ground, causing an explosive crash.

To minimize the chances of something going wrong, during takeoff the pilot coordinates the procedure with another crew member, usually the first officer, also called the copilot. As the plane travels down the runway accelerating for takeoff, the pilot focuses on the runway, making sure the path is clear; meanwhile, the first officer concentrates on the instrument control panel. When the plane reaches takeoff speed, the first officer immediately informs the pilot, who then pulls the nose of the plane up into the air.

Once the plane becomes airborne, the rest of the flight is usually easy unless extreme turbulence—shaking or bumping around of the plane—or poor weather is encountered. In flight, the pilot is assisted by the autopilot and flight management computer in steering the plane. Nevertheless, the pilot and first officer must continually check the control panel to ensure that all systems are working and that the fuel level remains sufficient. Once the plane reaches its destination, air traffic controllers guide the pilot in descending the plane toward the airport and onto the runway, where the pilot then taxis the plane to a dock or terminal. Throughout each procedure, pilots must maintain communication with air traffic control to be alert to other air traffic in the region and to important weather changes.

Weather Problems

Weather problems, whether clouds, precipitation, wind, or lightning, can pose the worst threats to airline pilots. Such weather problems can make it difficult to see the flight path and, at worst, make a pilot lose control of a jet. Captain X tells the story of his worst weather encounter:

> As our wheels left the ground [from the Cincinnati, Ohio, airport], there was a huge wall of black approaching. We got about a hundred feet up—and that's when the lightning started. . . . Things [electrical systems] started blowing, and we had to turn to our backup systems. The plane was encapsuled in a sheath of black fury. . . . This is when piloting becomes a questionable career choice. You're driving into rain at about 500 miles an hour. It's pounding on the glass less than two feet from your nostrils, and you can't see a thing because you can't use your windshield wipers. The sound on the roof is enough to drive you crazy. It's as if a thousand screaming furies were trying to scratch through the metal at you. . . . By then, most of our passengers were well beyond airsickness. They were clinging to their seats. They were scared, and justifiably. Everything unbattened [not fastened down] had begun to fly around the passenger cabin. . . . While that was going on, . . . my mind, trying to cope, was beginning to curl and fold in on itself. [The passengers] couldn't see what we were flying through. If they had been up here in front, they'd have been looking around for parachutes. It was like Frankenstein's lab—and we were the victims he was shooting voltage into. "Center, this is———!" I was shouting through

An airplane gets caught in a storm. Clouds, lightning, and other weather-related problems can be hazardous to airplanes.

the radio. Somewhere out there, there was an airport and a runway waiting. I had no idea where—all I could see was my instrument readings. But, wherever it was, it was time to get this airplane down there. Fortunately, about then, there was a clear spot ahead of us. We obtained a quick clearance and made a dive toward the runway. . . . Within seconds of touching we could feel the wall of the storm front hitting us.[7]

Fortunately, the weather is usually more cooperative than what this pilot encountered, but in foul weather or fair, piloting a jet full of passengers and cargo often calls for split-second decisions and a disciplined focus during each flight.

Working Conditions and Occupational Hazards

In order to fly a plane safely, a pilot must endure long periods of intense concentration. This frame of mind creates psychological stress because of the enormous responsibility of protecting the lives of the plane's passengers, sometimes hundreds of them. Exposure to this kind of stress can create fatigue in even the most dedicated pilot.

Besides the stress from being responsible for the safety of passengers and crew, pilots also suffer physical and psychological stress from

Crop duster pilots, like this one, experience risks others do not, including exposure to toxic chemicals.

other working conditions. Although by law pilots cannot fly more than one hundred hours per month, and on average most fly about eighty per month, jet lag and lack of sleep are common problems. Because flights can take place any time of day and any day of the year, most pilots work according to irregular schedules. This means they may work in the middle of the night, on weekends, or on holidays. About one-third of the time a pilot has an overnight layover and must stay in a hotel. Captain X tells what the pitfalls of being on such an irregular schedule are:

> We have to spend many nights in some anonymous motel room somewhere. We get up in the dark, we fumble around with our suitcases, and we have to try to pick clothes that will work in all temperature ranges. We're always getting colds. We're never certain what hour it is. In twenty years of flying, I've given up keeping my wristwatch current.[8]

Moreover, pilots may suffer stress from being away from home frequently. This can be especially problematic if a pilot is married and has children from whom separation is difficult. Captain X offers a glimpse of what life is like for a pilot's family through the words of his wife:

> The joke in our family is that my husband is "The Phantom." . . . He'll appear at the door. I haven't seen him

22

for weeks now. Suddenly he's home, and it's like being on a honeymoon. . . . Then off he goes again—and I'm left with PTA meetings. I shortcut the laundry. . . . The children and I will have Domino's Pizza orgies. It's a crazy kind of life, but it's the life that I'm used to. . . . It's the life of all airline people. And as for terrorists and thunderstorms and microbursts and takeoff crashes, I'm used to those worries. Over the years, I've become hardened to them.[9]

Long separations and constant worrying about the safety of airline pilots commonly causes depression in their spouses. About a third of airline couples suffer from marital stress, and the stress of being apart sometimes results in spouses seeking companionship through an extramarital affair. The level of stress in pilot marriages has resulted in a high divorce rate.

In addition to the general stresses of being a pilot, sometimes a particular job presents hazards specific to it. Crop dusters are exposed to toxic chemicals, and both agricultural and search-and-rescue pilots frequently must make dangerous landings in remote areas without a regular airstrip. Fire-fighting pilots are exposed to smoke, and those who track criminals may be at risk for personal injury from gunshot wounds, stabbings, or other physical attacks.

Earnings

Interestingly, the level of danger involved in a job does not determine the level of a pilot's pay—the size of the employer and seniority are the basis for pilot income. Because of the wide variety of jobs held by pilots, salaries differ greatly. In general, seniority is determined by how long a pilot has worked for an airline and by the type, size, and speed of the aircraft flown. The major airlines use many more jumbo jets that are faster and larger than the turboprops and commuter planes flown by regional or charter airlines. In addition, a pilot who is trained to fly many different types of aircraft is more valuable to an airline, and it will pay more to keep such a versatile professional. Airline pilots make the most, averaging $91,000 annually in 1998. However, most new hires start at the bottom and make much less than the average, but experienced pilots who serve as captains of large jets can make upwards of about $160,000. Pilots of charter lines, businesses, and other organizations may make substantially less. Beginners in charter lines sometimes start with pay as low as $15,000 a year.

Opportunities for Advancement

The substantially higher income that major airlines offer lures pilots from charter lines, businesses, or other employers. After logging several thousand hours in the air, pilots may apply for a job with a major airline as a first officer, an airline pilot that serves as second in com-

Women Pilots

This excerpt concerning women in aviation is from the official website of the Ninety-Nines, the oldest international organization for women pilots, and was written by pilot Kelli Gant.

Today, women pilots fly for the airlines, fly in the military and in space, fly air races, command helicopter mercy flights, haul freight, stock high mountain lakes with fish . . . teach students to fly, maintain jet engines, and transport corporate officers.

Blanch Scott was the first woman pilot, in 1910, when the plane that she was allowed to taxi mysteriously became airborne. In 1911, Harriet Quimby became the first licensed woman pilot. And later in 1912, Harriet became the first woman to fly across the English Channel. . . .

Phoebe Fairgrave Omelie was the first woman transport pilot. Phoebe, considered to be one of America's top women pilots in the 1920s and 1930s, developed a program for training women flight instructors and was appointed as Special Assistant for [the forerunner of NASA]. . . .

Willa Brown was the first African-American commercial pilot and first . . . in the Civil Air Patrol. . . . By 1930 there were 200 women pilots. . . . More than 935 women gained their licenses by . . . 1941. . . . As World War II progressed, women were able to break into many aspects of the aviation world. They served as ferry and test pilots, mechanics, flight controllers, instructors, and aircraft production line workers. At the beginning of 1943, 31.3 percent of the aviation work force were women. . . .

By the 1960s there were 12,400 licensed women pilots in the United States. . . . This number doubled by the end of the decade. Today, women comprise about 6 percent of pilots in the United States.

mand to a captain. A captain is the pilot first in command of an aircraft, who has advanced to this position through experience.

At major airlines, pilot promotions are based mostly on seniority and advanced training. With anywhere from five to fifteen years of experience, a first officer will advance to captain. Seniority is determined by length of service for the airline; for example, those who were hired three years ago have less seniority than pilots hired ten years ago. Captains can further advance their seniority by training to fly bigger, faster jets. Captain X explains promotions in the airlines:

> "Promotion," in our business, isn't the same as in other businesses. . . . Seniority is a determinant of your pay and of the schedules you get. It's also a criterion for who gets first crack at a job opening. There's also advancement by plane type and route structure. A jumbo-jet captain makes more than a [smaller craft] captain. A pilot flying to Europe makes more than a domestic pilot. . . . To rise in the ranks, you have to submit to more flight training. This is quite rigorous, and there are no guarantees accompanying it.[10]

In addition to the ongoing training pilots receive throughout their careers, many pilots are subject to various kinds of fitness tests required by their employers. For example, pilots who work for major airlines must pass psychological and aptitude tests that ensure the person in charge of a jet carrying 250 passengers is capable of making sound decisions in a split second under conditions of extreme stress. In addition, pilots are evaluated for physical fitness, undergo routine drug testing, and must demonstrate through periodic examinations that they are still proficient in flying.

Overall, despite the stress involved and the physical discomforts of living on an erratic schedule, most pilots love their jobs. Freeman summed up the reasons for this when he wrote,

> Flying an airplane is fun. Getting paid to do it is even better. For some people, it's the perfect job: an office that travels, a view that's constantly changing and challenges that are exhilarating. It has been said that a pilot's job is hours of boredom punctuated with seconds of sheer terror. This is perhaps hyperbole, but sometimes not all that far from the truth.[11]

Chapter 2

Flight Attendants

"Can I get you something to drink? Here's an extra pillow, sir. Can I get you anything else?" Every day thousands of airline passengers are served by a few men and women in airline uniforms. These uniformed persons are flight attendants, whose main responsibility is to ensure the comfort and safety of the flying public. Most flight attendants carry out this responsibility with relish because they enjoy working with people directly and find the day-to-day variety of the job invigorating. Former flight attendant Wendy Stafford explains, "No one can say for sure just what the charm of a flight attendant is. But I remember the look on a young man's face on one of my flights. He . . . gazed up at me with wonder, and asked, 'Is this what you do for your job—meet people and fly to different places all the time? Cool.'"[12]

Nevertheless, the work of a flight attendant can sometimes be difficult and tiring. To most of the flying public, flight attendants represent the airline with which they are flying. It is therefore extremely important for flight attendants to be able to keep their cool at all times and to be friendly to passengers even when they themselves are tired or when passengers are outright rude to them. Stafford says that "those of us who fly know that in reality the job is hard work, sometimes with long hours and grouchy customers. It is difficult to find the glamour in your job when you are down on your hands and knees in the galley [food preparation area], going through tray carriers looking for someone's lower dentures they left on a tray!"[13]

Flight attendants must also be able to deal with passengers who are behaving violently or irrationally, keeping them under control and from harming themselves or other passengers. Elliot Neal Hester, a flight attendant for thirteen years, describes an incident

26

that demonstrates the typical way a flight attendant deals with rude passengers:

About an hour after take-off . . . a loud, somewhat primordial scream ripped through the cabin [the part of a plane where passengers are seated]. It sounded as if a large, carnivorous animal had escaped from the cargo hold and was terrorizing passengers at the rear of the airplane. When I swung around, I realized I was only half right. A wild-eyed male passenger was terrorizing passengers at the rear of the plane. His arms flailed, his head jerked spasmodically—he looked like the deranged criminal in a low-budget biker flick. . . .

A flight attendant serves a drink to a passenger, one of her many responsibilities.

Slowly I walked toward the irate passenger. . . . The problem passenger was in a row by himself, sitting in the middle seat. I stopped, stared at him and smiled. Dressed in blue jeans and a tattered blue jean jacket, frizzy hair cascading past his shoulders, he looked up at me with eyes as wild as Borneo. "Can I get you something to eat? Sir?" His eyes crawled from my shoes to the crown of my freshly shaven head, looking for a reason to launch an attack. "Nawww," he said. "But I'll have another Jack Daniel's and a beer." On his tray table there were three empty Jack Daniel's minis and a crumpled can of Budweiser. "I don't think that's a very good idea," I said. "How about a Coke?" He glared at me . . . gave me one final, I'm-gonna-kill-you look, then turned to the window. . . . As soon as I rejoined my serving partner, the irate passenger screamed [obscenities] at a volume that . . . was heard all the way to the cockpit. . . . Herein lies the problem of potentially violent airline passengers: At 30,000 feet, you can't call a cop. Nor can you throw a guy out the door. . . . I returned to the back of the plane and, using a calm, non-combative voice, I confronted the passenger again. "Sir, please try to calm down," I said. "There's no need to get upset and there's certainly no reason to use profanity." [More obscenities followed.] At this point, I . . . turned to Donna, my . . . colleague. . . . "Sir, please . . . " she said, settling her warm, motherly gaze upon him. "Can you just lower your voice a bit?" He lashed her with insults too degrading to repeat. But when Donna had finally had enough, she reached for the interphone and called the cockpit.[14]

Fortunately, this passenger was subdued and arrested when the plane landed at its destination.

A Flight Attendant's Day

On a long flight, being pleasant to passengers while battling fatigue and aching legs from hours of standing and walking in the plane's cabin can be quite a challenge. Serving drinks and getting extras for passengers are only a few of the duties flight attendants must perform. Before a routine flight, they must first check the cabin to ensure that all safety and convenience materials are adequately stocked onboard. This includes checking that each seat has an oxy-

Heroic Flight Attendants

Over the years many flight attendants have risked their lives to protect their passengers. Perhaps one of the most courageous acts of a flight attendant was that of Francis Cabel of Phillipines Airlines in January 2001.

When Flight 812 en route from Davao City to Manila was hijacked by Reginald Chua, Cabel went to the cockpit to help. "At the flight deck door, I saw (Chua) and he saw me," Cabel recalled, according to the *Philippine Daily Inquirer.* "He poked his gun against my forehead and said, (we will all die). . . . His eyes were sharp. He meant business." However, Cabel, who noticed Chua was also clutching a grenade, responded with quick thinking. He asked Chua what was wrong and the hijacker responded that the problem was money. Cabel gave all his cash to the hijacker and then collected more from passengers.

Then Chua demanded that the rear door in the passenger cabin be opened so he could jump wearing a homemade parachute. Cabel was the only one strong enough and not flying the plane who could open that door while in flight. However, he knew that, opening the door at 6,000 feet at a speed of just over 300 miles per hour, he would likely be sucked outside. Cabel recalled, "It was a gamble I had to make. If I don't do it, we'd all die. And so at gunpoint, I grabbed the operating handle, pulled it open and closed my eyes." When the door opened Cabel clung to a shoulder harness by the door, but the air pressure blew his feet upwards. Meanwhile, Chua had stuck his head out the door and consequently had his head and chest forced against the outside of the plane while his legs and torso were bent around the opening inside. Cabel said, "He . . . was still clutching the grenade. When I saw that, I feared it might explode. So I immediately pushed [him] off the plane. It was a split-moment decision." The hijacker fell to his death without ever opening his parachute.

gen mask and a seat belt, that there are enough pillows and blankets for all passengers, and also that the appropriate number of meals, snacks, and drinks are supplied on the plane. During boarding, flight attendants check tickets, greet passengers, and help them store baggage or find their seats. Once all passengers are on board, prior to

Flight attendants stock a beverage cart in preparation for a flight.

takeoff, flight attendants instruct passengers in safety and emergency procedures. They also check to make sure all passengers have their seat belts on whenever the seat-belt sign is lit, which is usually while taking off, climbing into the sky, descending, landing, and during times of extreme turbulence. During the flight, attendants serve refreshments, distribute convenience items such as pillows or blankets, and collect trash.

Flight attendants also often have routine ground duties. Many make public relations appearances for their airline, either to attract passengers or to recruit employees. Once a month, during one of the four-day periods when she is not in flight, Kelly Lange participates in a conference that is put on by several airlines, including hers, and that is designed to introduce both small companies and larger corporations to the technological and convenience advances of their airlines in order to generate business. The presentation could include the use of phones on planes or a discount program offered to corporations who fly a lot of employees on business. Lange, along with other flight attendants, pilots, and other airline representatives, helps present the information by giving talks and by presenting diagrams, charts, or pictures to illustrate important points. Most ground duties, however, involve report writing and documentation. As part of the normal routine, flight attendants must write a report to the captain detailing any occurrences of medical problems or disruptions with passengers during each flight.

Sometimes, however, things do not go according to the normal routine. At these times it is important for flight attendants to be able to keep a calm, clear head when under pressure so they can deal quickly and appropriately with problems or emergencies. They reassure frightened passengers during turbulent conditions, direct passengers during emergency landings and evacuations, and administer first aid to injured or ill passengers during the flight. This report by a flight attendant records the details of dealing with a sick passenger during a flight:

> Pax [passenger] walked out of lavatory [rest room], urinated in pants, and grabbed seat back, hand shaking, on [left] side. I asked, "OK?" Pax responded, "No, I feel dizzy." I immediately assisted him into the seat. He was rigid, unable to sit up straight, short of breath, eyes rolled back, foam from mouth—all within 90 seconds. Flight attendant came with medical kit. . . . I called [captain] and paged for doctor on board. . . . Flight attendant started oxygen and doctor took pulse and blood pressure.[15]

Thanks to the quick action of the flight attendants, this passenger, who suffered from a lack of oxygen and heart problems caused by emphysema (abnormal expansion of air spaces in the lungs) and exaggerated by being at a high altitude, survived.

Working Conditions: Stress Plus Pleasure

Due to the nature of their job responsibilities, flight attendants are subjected to a great deal of emotional and physical stress. The pressure to act friendly and stay calm in the face of unpleasant and sometimes disturbing circumstances can exact a toll on some flight attendants. After a few years of such intense emotional self-control some flight attendants suffer from burnout and quit.

In addition to the emotional stress of the job, there may be risks to physical health. Respiratory problems may arise from working in the pressurized environment of an airplane cabin and breathing recycled air. Flight attendants may also suffer from fatigue as a result of irregular sleep patterns that are caused by intermittent work schedules. Sudden bursts of turbulence can knock a flight attendant down or against obstructions in the cabin, causing injuries. In addition, many flight attendants suffer from head and back injuries when overhead compartment doors swing open on them. Phil Guzman, a flight attendant in his seventh year of service, was working a flight en route from Chicago to New York City when the plane was jolted by a sudden jab of turbulence at thirty thousand feet. He and two other flight attendants were flung down in the aisle as they were serving meals to passengers. As he was gripping the seat to stand up, Guzman noticed the meal cart begin to roll toward him. He jumped out of the way just in time, but at that very moment the plane was rocked by more turbulence, and the door of the baggage compartment directly above Guzman's head popped open, thumping him on the back of his head and knocking him out cold. Fortunately, he recovered with only a bad headache and a bump on the head.

Stress and discomfort are not, however, the only outcomes of the job of being a flight attendant. There are positive outcomes as well. In addition to meeting lots of people from many different places, flight attendants have the opportunity to travel all over the country—or even the world, if they work for an international airline. Wendy Stafford, president of Airline Inflight Resources and a former flight attendant, says,

> The mere mention of the flight attendant job conjures up images of jetting away to an exotic Caribbean Island or spending a week skiing in the majestic Alps. Of course the job itself is not always glamorous, but most people do not possess the mobility of the flight attendant to see the world while they are still young enough to enjoy it.[16]

Sometimes layovers, which can last as little as a couple of hours to as long as a couple of days, allow flight attendants some free time to sightsee in places like San Francisco, Washington, D.C., or even Rome, Paris, or Hong Kong.

Of course, the same schedules that allow flight attendants to travel all over the world also add up to a great deal of time spent away from home. On average, flight attendants spend anywhere from one-third to one-half of their time away from home in flight or at hotels during layovers. Such schedules may cause marital or family stress and are a primary reason why many flight attendants leave their jobs. For instance, Donna Bemelman had been a flight attendant for eight

The History of the Flight Attendant Position

The earliest "cabin attendants" were young men who lifted luggage, helped people onto the plane, and reassured nervous fliers. In 1930 Ellen Church, a nurse, suggested that Boeing Air Transport hire registered nurses as attendants because they could help with anyone who got sick during flight. Boeing hired eight nurses, and the position of "airline stewardess" was born. These stewardesses served sandwiches and water to passengers and passed out gum to ease pressure in the ears. During the 1940s the nursing requirement was dropped, and the stewardess position became popular among young single women.

Until the 1970s and 1980s most airlines had strict standards for stewardesses. They had to keep a certain weight in proportion to height and wore form-fitting uniforms and high heels. These women, who were underpaid with few benefits, usually lost their jobs when they married. During the 1960s some airlines hired men and changed the name of the position to "flight attendant." By the 1980s unions helped change the strict standards of the job, doing away with the weight restriction and gaining better pay and benefits. Today men and women, single or married, many with children, enjoy careers as flight attendants.

An airline stewardess in 1945. The airline stewardess position became popular with young women during the 1940s.

years and had gained through seniority a regular route, but one that required her to be gone four consecutive days out of every week. She spent much of the three days she was at home catching up on her sleep and recovering from jet lag. Although at first this seemed merely to be a slight inconvenience for doing the job she loved, several years after she married and had two children, her absences and tiredness began to wear on her and her family. Recognizing that she wanted to spend more time with her children while they were young and realizing that she and her husband were rapidly becoming strangers living in the same place, Bemelman made the decision to leave her job as a flight attendant.

Rather than quit as Bemelman did, some flight attendants choose to cut back on their flight time because they want to maintain their seniority. There are many who work part time, perhaps flying two weeks out of the month and then spending the rest of the time at home.

Becoming a Flight Attendant

It takes a great deal of emotional and physical stress to prompt a flight attendant to leave behind a job in which so much training has been invested. To minimize turnover rates, the airlines are very discriminatory in whom they choose to hire as flight attendants, preferring those who speak a foreign language and have a degree in psychology, education, or public relations, although minimum requirements are for a high school diploma. Having experience in these fields better prepares a person for the rigorous training program and the subsequent responsibilities of being a flight attendant. Marianne Moore, a U.S. Air flight attendant with sixteen years' experience, explains: "Very intensive training is necessary to become a flight attendant. First of all, over the years, it's become a lot more popular job, and the airline companies go through a big screening process in selecting the applicants who will go through training school."[17]

The training period, which may last anywhere from three to nine weeks, is rigorous and very fast paced. Trainees attend classes in food service; emergency procedures in cases such as fire, depressurization, or a crash; and strategies for dealing with hijackers. They must learn FAA regulations and familiarize themselves with each type of aircraft and its safety equipment. In simulators, they practice evacuating an airplane under various conditions, and they are trained to administer first aid. All trainees are evaluated on a regular basis. A veteran pilot who is married to a former flight attendant describes the experience of training school:

They have to learn about evacuation techniques. The doors on a plane are extraordinarily dangerous. They weigh hundreds of pounds, and they're "armed" with escape chutes. They can break you in two if you don't know what you're doing with them. It's not just the skills—you have to learn to *command* people. . . . They've got to get some big [guy to move] off a seat cushion and

Flight attendants practice evacuating passengers from a smoke-filled flight simulator.

help them free up an exit or else they're all going to perish in there. . . . When they get through with that, and they've learned about food service—(you think you know cooking? —you've got a couple of surprises coming: try to rustle up eggs when you're at 40,000 feet; the things will turn green; this is a whole different environment you're dealing with)—when you've learned about that, you'll get to . . . try to inflate a life raft that's about the size of three elephants. Forget about swimsuits—you're going to do this with your street clothes on. And you're going to do it in water, and sometimes at night, and sometimes when it's freezing out.[18]

Although trainees sometimes are given a weekly allowance to pay for accommodations and meals during the training period, they are not considered employees of the airline until they complete the training program and pass all of the tests. Even then, the new employees must fly several practice flights before they are scheduled as regular employees.

Moving on Up

Once hired by an airline, a flight attendant spends the first year or two flying on what is called "reserve." Flight attendants on reserve do not have a regular preplanned schedule and usually do not know where or when they will be flying from day to day, as one pilot explains:

> When a flight attendant's hired, she'll [or he'll] be bestowed with a seniority number. This will dictate . . . pay and . . . rank. . . . The higher [the] number, the less popular the flights she'll [or he'll] garner. . . . Forget San Francisco. She's [or he's] going to get those 2 a.m. Oshkosh beauties. Depending on the airline, there may be flights that will be barred. . . . Certain great flights will be controlled by the senior people. No younger [flight attendant] is going to fly to Nairobi; there are just too many seniors waiting in line to see Safari Country.[19]

Flight attendants move off the reserve list when attendants who have more seniority are promoted to other types of positions, retire, or quit. Only then may flight attendants gain a regular schedule, flying the same routes, or lines, from week to week. Sometimes, each month the regular schedules must be bid (an attempt to win by requesting), with the best lines usually going to those flight attendants with the greatest seniority, those who have worked for the airline the longest.

In the major airlines, experienced flight attendants may sometimes be promoted to head attendant, also called a purser, who oversees all of the other flight attendants on a flight. The purser is also responsible for managing inventory, such as meals and beverages; tallying up alcohol sales during a flight; and solving problems with staff and service equipment. Some flight attendants are promoted to supervisor with the responsibility of recruiting and training new hires for the airline.

Nevertheless, regardless of seniority or experience, all flight attendants must receive ongoing training from year to year. The purpose of the training is to keep flight attendants abreast of the latest strategies or technology in emergency procedures or public relations and to keep their working knowledge fresh. Moore says,

> Once a year we have to go through recurrent training and learn anything new that's come out. . . . We have to practice emergency procedures, including a mock exercise in evacuating an airplane. You get into the simulator and go to your exit and sometimes the exit will be blocked by fire and you have to know what to do in that situation. . . . [We also are] required to go through eight hours of hijack training.[20]

A flight attendant (right) participates in a fire drill. Regardless of experience, all flight attendants must take part in ongoing training sessions.

Earnings

Training, however, does not dictate the pay scale—it simply secures employment. In general, the more financially stable the airline company is, the better the pay is. The national average is about $30,000 annually, although flight attendants with a lot of seniority may earn as much as $50,000 a year. However, with so many bigger airlines swallowing up smaller lines in mergers and buyouts, future job stability for flight attendants is uncertain. Moore notes that "you have to be flexible. That's the name of the game. You might be told one day—or you might just pick up a newspaper and find out—that your airline was bought by somebody else, which more than likely means you'll have a move on your hands. You have to go where the flying is."[21]

Despite the increasing instability of the airline industry, each year there are thousands more aspiring flight attendants than there are actual jobs available. Those who stick with the job are there because they love all kinds of people and the changes in their daily routines. Moore sums up her job by saying, "You have to realize that it's not all a glamour job. You do get to work with the public and you can get a lot of fulfillment by the things you do for your passengers, but it's hard and tedious work, and it's very uncertain these days."[22]

Chapter 3

Air Traffic Controllers

The dark room is filled with dim figures hurriedly darting between the green glowing screens of flashing information. This is not a scene from a suspense movie but rather the real-life drama of that icon of airline safety—the air traffic controller. Frantic though their work may be, air traffic controllers enjoy the fast-paced intensity, the sense of contribution, and the challenge of meeting the demands of the job, as the author of an air traffic control (ATC) book explains:

> It was the sense of exhilaration, of satisfaction, of knowing that he had done a good job or a not-so-good job when the day was done. Another equated it with playing a video game—and getting paid to play the game. Others voiced the sense of contributing to pilot, plane, and passenger wellbeing, whether through radar and radio or giving preflight briefings over the phone.[23]

Directing Planes

It is important that air traffic controllers love their jobs because they are the specially trained professionals who are responsible for the safe and efficient operation of aircraft both at the airport and while flying in airspace between ports. This responsibility is one of the most important in aviation. Without air traffic controllers planes would not be able to know if they were on a collision course with other aircraft or if sudden weather changes were ahead. There would be no one for lost planes to contact for help. The results could be devastating: Many more planes would crash and more people would die. In short, air traffic controllers keep flying safe.

Besides ensuring safety, air traffic controllers are under a great deal of pressure to make planes stick to tight flight schedules. Their job, then, is a balancing act of packing as many planes as possible into a designated airspace and yet making sure all of those planes stay safely separated in the air. In addition, air traffic controllers must direct planes to land as quickly as possible, making sure that the previous plane has taxied off the active runway out of the way of new arrivals.

How exactly do air traffic controllers make flying both safe and efficient? If planes are close enough to the air traffic control tower or facility where the controller works, then visual observation can be used to monitor planes. Controllers also use various technological tools, including radar that tracks the progress and whereabouts of planes. Radar is a device that sends out radio waves that reflect off objects in its vicinity. The device registers the location of the object and its direction of movement and speed. When controllers send out a radar sweep, any aircraft in their airspace will show up on the green radar screen as a tiny blip. Another radar device, called an interrogator, "asks" an aircraft's transponder (a radio or radar tool that receives and emits signals) to respond. This response is recorded in the ATC tower and tells the controller what kind of aircraft the blip is and identifies it by individual name or number.

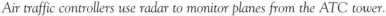

Air traffic controllers use radar to monitor planes from the ATC tower.

Once the controller can positively identify an aircraft and knows its direction and speed, the pilot of the aircraft can be contacted by radio. The controller guides the pilot through the landing process by giving step-by-step directions. The following interchange is an example of how a controller guides planes into safe landings:

[Pilot]: Kansas City Approach, Cherokee Eight Five One Five November.

[ATC]: *Cherokee Eight Five One Five November, Kansas City Approach, go ahead.*

[Pilot]: Approach, Cherokee Eight Five One Five November is over Lake Perry at five thousand five hundred, landing International with Bravo.

[ATC]: *Cherokee One Five November, squawk zero two six three and ident.*

[Pilot]: Roger, zero two six three. Cherokee One Five November.

[ATC]: *Cherokee One Five November, radar contact.*

[Pilot waits until ATC gives clearance to enter the airport.]

[ATC]: *Cherokee One Five November, cleared into the TCA.* [24]

Controllers visually monitor a plane during takeoff.

A Profile of the FAA

The Federal Aviation Administration (FAA) is an agency of the U.S. Department of Transportation, and was established in 1958. Its primary responsibility is for the safety of civil aviation. To fulfill this responsibility, it makes and enforces aviation rules and ensures that aircraft manufacturing and maintenance standards are met. The FAA also licenses pilots and aircraft mechanics.

Besides managing the air traffic control system, the FAA also builds and maintains navigational aids such as radar systems, registers aircraft, provides flight insurance, and records ownership titles to aircraft. In addition, the agency develops and implements aircraft noise control programs and evaluates other ways aviation affects the environment, including the presence of jet fuel exhaust in the air. The FAA regulates the commercial space industry, licensing space launch facilities and space payloads (the goods being transported, such as a commercial satellite used for cell phones or television).

In this process, first the controller acknowledges the transmission from the pilot. Then the permission to approach the airport is given, followed by a request for the pilot to identify the aircraft. Once the aircraft has been identified on the radar screen, the controller acknowledges this, and then if there is no other traffic or barriers, the controller gives clearance to the pilot to land the plane. Throughout the process the controller expects the pilot to repeat the directions as a confirmation that they have been received and understood correctly.

Managing the Busy Skies

Controllers also use the information they receive from radar to warn pilots about other aircraft in their vicinity. If it appears that two or more planes are moving in close to each other, the controller must quickly figure out where to redirect the aircraft to avoid a collision. To accomplish this a controller must be able to form a mental picture of the traffic pattern needed for all of the planes in that airspace to keep a safe distance apart while moving. For example, in front of him [a New York City controller] is a screen that's about to snarl in a logjam. There are seventeen planes headed straight for a collision, and he has about ninety-five seconds in which to get all their vectors [orders for changes in direction] sorted. But hey, man, no problem. He starts rattling commands at them. He'll tell two to turn left. He'll tell three to reduce airspeed. He'll tell this guy to climb, he'll tell that guy to drop a bit, and the pilots will respond with rarely a question as to the reason for it. . . . The object of the exercise is to try to keep all those airplanes separated. At any given time, there may be 600 planes to follow. At a center like this, you have to maintain five miles of air separation. If you violate that, you'll have some interesting things come down on you.[25]

A violation such as this is called a "deal," and each time a deal occurs the controller has to explain what happened and the incident goes down forever on record. A controller who commits three deals within two and a half years is required to undergo a rigorous retraining period and, if necessary, is transferred to a less busy ATC center.

Weather Problems

Besides managing air traffic patterns, air traffic controllers also brief departing pilots on current weather conditions and weather predictions along the route and at the destination. As planes come and go through airspace, controllers update pilots on current weather conditions to keep them abreast of any possible changes since takeoff.

However, when the weather itself turns dreadful, the controller may be a pilot's only hope for survival. One pilot of a jumbo jet who was caught in violent thunderstorms in the midst of forming tornadoes called the air traffic controller "my lifeline and savior. I was out there in space and there was just the sound of his voice to tether me."[26] Another pilot of a small plane wound up stuck in snowy skies and became worried about ice forming on the wings, which can cause a plane to plummet to the ground. In poor visibility the pilot, who was not certified to fly by instruments, sent out a distress signal to air traffic control. The air traffic controller who responded was able to clear the pilot to land at an airport close to where he was flying. Unfortunately, in order to get to the runway the pilot would have to fly near a restricted area where the military was testing explosives. The controller contacted the military to have the testing suspended and then was able to guide the pilot to the runway.

In helping an aircraft in distress, that controller was following an important rule. Even in the midst of monitoring hundreds of other planes, the controller's first responsibility is always to an aircraft in distress, whether the distress results from mechanical failure, hijacking, getting lost, or, most commonly, adverse weather conditions. In addition to helping distressed planes, controllers must be alert to missing or downed aircraft and coordinate searches when needed. One air traffic controller near Grand Junction, Colorado, was watching the blips on her screen when suddenly one of them disappeared. Unable to establish contact with the aircraft, the controller alerted the facility manager to the situation. He also tried to establish contact but to no avail. Determining that the plane had dropped off the radarscope over the foothills and near the looming peaks of the Rocky Mountains, ATC initiated a search for the missing aircraft. Eventually search-and-rescue flight teams located the plane in an open field within the foothills, where it had made an emergency landing after experiencing engine failure and discovering that the radio was inoperative.

Technical Difficulties

Unfortunately, air traffic control itself is not immune to mechanical and technical failures. When radar screens go blank or tower radios break, controllers are left scrambling to find another way of communicating with the pilots in their airspace. Situations like this can nearly send a controller to the madhouse as the experience of a Newark, New Jersey, controller shows:

Lightning bolts and other adverse weather conditions can cause a controller's equipment to fail.

A few years ago, a controller guiding 10 jets in a great curving arc toward Newark suddenly lost his frequency just as he had to turn the pilots onto the final approach to the runway. Watching in helpless horror as his planes careened farther and farther off course, the controller rose from his chair with an animal scream, burst into a sweat and began tearing off his shirt. By the time radio contact was re-established—and the errant planes were reined in—the controller was quivering on the floor half-naked, and was discharged on a medical leave until he could regain his wits.[27]

Equipment failures are largely the result of the FAA's slow pace in modernizing the computer and communication systems, some of which are twenty or thirty years old. Although equipment failures have yet to cause any midair collisions between aircraft, the number of near misses due to such failures has been rising in recent years, especially in airspace near the nation's busiest airports.

The New FAA Air Traffic Control System

Although performing all of the responsibilities of an air traffic controller simultaneously and accurately is a minute-by-minute challenge, the job may become a little easier during the 2010s, when the FAA implements a new automated air traffic control system. The new system will utilize powerful computers that will assume some of the controllers' duties, easing the demands of high air traffic, especially at the busiest airports. The computers will determine how far apart planes should be and will lay out safe and efficient traffic patterns for controllers to relay to pilots. In addition, the old green radar screens will be replaced with full-color computer workstations that will allow controllers to choose radio channels for pilot communications by touching buttons on the monitor screen rather than the present method of turning dials and pressing switches. Controllers will also be able to zoom in on sections of their assigned airspace, allowing them to get a closer look at moving traffic.

A Stressful Job

Equipment failure is not the only source of stress for a controller on the job, however. The very nature of the job can cause considerable stress—the intensity, the lightning pace, the knowledge that at every second the lives of hundreds of people depend on a job done exactly right. The work of a controller is also a juggling act, requiring attention to several different tasks at one time, as the daily routine for this Newark controller illustrates:

> Between issuing commands, Zack [Tom Zaccheo] listens for each pilot to read back his instructions; asks a nearby controller if he can "borrow" some airspace for one of his planes; coordinates, over an outside telephone line, a tricky landing with the Newark tower, and writes down on individual "flight strips" every altitude and speed he gives to pilots. If Zack's radar goes down . . . those flight strips are the only way a supervisor, running to bail him out, can figure out which way his planes are headed.[28]

To perform all of those tasks correctly and simultaneously, a controller must be able to maintain long periods of intense concentration.

Although such concentration can be draining, it is necessary to ensure the safety of planes in flight. Because there are so many things happening at once, all at a furious pace, even a momentary lapse in attention can potentially cause major problems. For example, a controller in Newark describes creating a mental picture of the traffic pattern and giving directions to pilots smoothly and quickly, but then, "his mind wanders—don't forget to pick up milk on the way home— and suddenly he looks back at the scope and it's gone: no picture, no pattern, just a mad spray of blips . . . heading—where? . . . He can't remember, and though he tries to catch up, he's already behind, conflicts arising faster than he can react."[29]

The stress of the job is sometimes compounded by lots of overtime hours, although generally this is true at only the busiest airspace facilities, such as New York; Newark; Washington, D.C.; Chicago; Los Angeles; and a host of others. Although most controllers work forty-hour workweeks with occasional overtime, the busier facilities may make overtime routine. And because traffic is in the air twenty-four hours a day, seven days a week, somebody has to be there giving commands at, for example, 3:00 A.M. on a Saturday morning. Most controllers work in day, evening, or night shifts and alternate

A controller works the evening shift, monitoring overnight flights.

weekends and holidays. Jim Hunter, a Newark controller, often works a 3:00 P.M. to 11:00 P.M. shift followed by a 7:00 A.M. to 3:00 P.M. shift the next day. There have even been days he worked these hours and then, because the tower was short staffed, followed up with an extra shift until midnight. Hunter says of the fatigue he experiences from too much overtime, "I drive home and barely remember the trip. I'm on the couch. I look around: Wow, I'm home! How'd that happen?"[30]

The demands of being an air traffic controller can cause both mental and physical problems for some people in this profession. A visit to a psychiatrist is not uncommon among air traffic controllers. Some controllers have developed nervous symptoms such as twitches while others are simply tired all the time.

Selection and Training: Who Is Right for This Job?

The demands of an air traffic controller's job call for a special kind of personality. Most air traffic controllers are people who have a huge need for achievement and who thrive in a position in which they make decisions and solve problems independently. The FAA listed necessary traits in its ATC career brochure: "You have to be able to think abstractly, especially at the Center. You have to do first things first, establish priorities. You have to have automatic recall. You have to look at errors objectively and reconstruct situations. You have to accept the responsibilities of the job."[31] In addition, controllers must be capable of great self-control and quick learning, and possess patience, planning abilities, and good communication skills.

The FAA begins the process of identifying qualified applicants who possess these traits through a written test. Offered by the Federal Civil Service system, the test measures skills in abstract reasoning and spatial visualization, among other areas. Those who pass the test then go for a week of screening at the FAA Academy in Oklahoma City, Oklahoma, where they take more aptitude tests using computerized simulators and undergo both physical and psychological examinations.

Once applicants pass both the written test and the screening process, training at the FAA Academy begins. Trainees spend the first seven months becoming familiar with ATC equipment and learning the fundamentals of the airway system, FAA regulations, and aircraft performance. After completing the training they must pass more tests in order to be employed at an ATC facility. The tests measure speed and accuracy in recognizing and solving air traffic problems using FAA rules and procedures.

Even after passing the training tests, a new air traffic controller must experience yet more training, this time on the job, before advancing to full controller responsibilities. The type of training received depends on the type of ATC facility where the controller works.

Tower Centers

There are basically three different types of ATC facilities, each of which represents a link in the process of guiding an airplane from takeoff to landing. It is easiest to understand what a controller's responsibilities are at each facility in terms of this process.

The first part of any flight begins with the takeoff and ascent, directed from the airport control tower where tower or terminal controllers coordinate the movement of air traffic in and out of airports. This includes ensuring that planes keep a safe distance apart while departing from the airport. Tower controllers may play one of three roles, depending on their level of experience.

When first assigned to a tower facility, a new hire will start out in the position of ground controller and will be responsible for directing the plane to the proper runway. The ground controller watches the planes from the tower and directs them to the runway,

47

making sure that they do not cross active runways where other planes are taking off or landing.

A ground controller may advance with experience to the position of local controller. The local controller gives a pilot the most current information on weather, wind speed and direction, and visibility. The local controller also gives a pilot clearance for takeoff from the directed runway.

Finally, when the plane has taken off and is making its ascent, the departure controller—the most advanced tower position—guides the pilot out of the airport. Departure controllers are also responsible for directing the traffic pattern to keep planes safely separated in the air up to a forty-mile radius around the airport.

En Route Centers

Once the plane is in the air, the tower controllers notify en route controllers who work at an en route facility within the plane's flight path. There are twenty-one en route control centers spread out across the nation, each of which is responsible for a particular section of airspace. Within the assigned airspace are many different flight routes, any of which might have planes flying along them at any given time. En route controllers work in teams of three, and each team is responsible for a section of the center's assigned airspace and the planes on routes within that airspace. This could mean, for

On the recommendation of the ATC, an airplane taxis to a runway in preparation for takeoff.

En route controllers use radar to monitor airspace.

example, that a team is responsible for planes between forty to one hundred miles south of the center and flying at altitudes between twelve thousand and twenty thousand feet.

A team is made up of a radar controller, who is the senior team member, and two assistant radar controllers, who manage traffic in their airspace and coordinate with other teams at the center as planes progress along their routes. When a plane leaves the airport airspace, a tower controller sends a copy of the flight plan to the proper en route center, where an associate radar controller—usually the least experienced one—collects it and organizes it along with scores of other flight plans for all of the planes that will be entering the en route center team's airspace. The flight plans are then delivered to the radar controller, who assumes responsibility for the plane from the tower controller as the plane enters the new airspace.

While a plane is within a team's airspace, the radar controller is responsible for observing the plane on radar, ensuring that it keeps safe distances from other aircraft, and directing the pilot to make changes in altitude or direction when conflicting flight paths make such changes necessary to avoid a collision. The radar controller also warns pilots about bad weather or other potential hazards. Sometimes a pilot will request a change of direction or altitude due to weather problems, and the radar controller checks to see if the proposed

49

A plane descends toward a runway deemed safe by the arrival controller.

change will interfere with any other planes in flight. If it is safe, the radar controller will clear the pilot to make the requested change.

As the plane progresses along its flight path, it continually enters and exits different airspace sections for that en route center. When it leaves one section, the radar controller will pass the flight plan and responsibility for that plane on to the team responsible for the next section that the plane will be flying through. When a plane leaves one en route center's airspace and enters the assigned airspace of another en route center, the last team at the previous center will pass on the flight plan to the proper team at the new center, which then assumes responsibility for the plane.

Flight Service Stations and the End of the Journey

Within the airspace of the twenty-one en route centers all over the country are one hundred flight service stations that employ controllers who provide a supplementary role but do not actively manage flight traffic. Flight service specialists give pilots information on their assigned airspace section, including terrain, weather, and suggested route changes. They also help pilots in an emergency and are responsible for coordinating searches for missing or overdue aircraft.

When a plane finally gets close to its destination, the en route controller will notify the arrival controller at the tower center of the airport where the plane will be landing. Thus, the procedure of controlling a flight comes full circle, ending up where it began—at a tower center, except that it is at a different airport this time. The arrival controller will coordinate the traffic flow within the airport's airspace until the plane gets close enough to start its descent. At this point the arrival controller will clear the pilot to descend or, if the airport is extremely busy, will fit the plane into a traffic pattern with other planes waiting to land. This could mean asking the pilot to change speed or circle above the airport to delay the landing until previous planes have had a chance to land and taxi off the runway. When the arrival controller determines it is safe for a plane to land, the pilot is cleared to descend toward an assigned runway.

Once the plane has landed, the local controller guides the plane off the runway, and the ground controller directs the plane as it taxis toward the appropriate terminal gate. At any given time all controllers may be observing and directing many planes, giving pilots information about weather and organizing the traffic pattern in their minds.

Earnings and Benefits

With so many competing duties and the pressure to perform perfectly, the job of an air traffic controller is undoubtedly one of the most challenging in the field of aeronautics. The immense responsibilities of controllers are reflected in the pay they receive. While the average income in 1998 was just over $48,000 annually, at some of the busiest airports' experienced controllers earned as much as $87,000 per year.

However, air traffic controllers do what they do not for the money but because they have a need for the challenge and excitement their job offers them. Newark tower controller Jim Hunter explains why he loves his job, harried though it is:

> I'm sure there's long-term effects of working so much traffic. . . . But right now I don't see it. I always say, "There isn't enough traffic out there to put me down." Actually, I get a buzz off it. It's true. . . . I come back [from breaks] five minutes early to get the busy scope. . . . Or I'll tell my supes [supervisors] to combine two radar positions for me. At the end of a busy shift, I'll be like: "They shut off the overflow runway! I was crushed with traffic! It was great!"[32]

Chapter 4

Aircraft Mechanics

Without aircraft mechanics, planes would not fly. Airplanes are basically large machines that break down sometimes and have to be fixed. Like an automobile, they stay in operation longer and work more reliably when they are regularly maintained. Aircraft mechanics are the caretakers of planes and helicopters.

Aircraft mechanics are, however, unlike any other mechanic because of the heavy responsibility they have for ensuring the safety of airplane passengers and crew. When an airplane breaks down, the result is usually tragic. A missing bolt could mean engine failure, sending a jumbo jet plummeting to the ground; inoperative instruments could misguide a pilot into a collision with another aircraft during takeoff. In either situation, people will die.

Despite the responsibility of ensuring safety, aircraft mechanics love their jobs. Many mechanics enjoy the challenge of solving an aircraft's mechanical and electrical problems. They also possess a certain amount of awe for flying machines, especially the biggest and fastest airplanes. Adam Traynor, an aircraft mechanic for a company in Canada, sums up what he considers to be the challenge and the attraction in his profession:

> The largest factor in my desire to become a gas turbine engine overhaul technician [of airplanes] was pride in knowing that the work I would do would mean the difference between life and death for the 450 people taking off in that 747 (an aircraft which I had always found truly awesome— watching one take off still gives me goose bumps) and knowing that I had a part with the maintenance of the motive force of a machine that defies gravity.[33]

Of course, not every aircraft mechanic is responsible for a 747 jumbo jet—many work with smaller aircraft—but all mechanics are skilled professionals who perform emergency repairs, scheduled maintenance, and inspections of aircraft, all of which must be carried out according to FAA safety regulations. Most aircraft mechanics specialize in one or two areas of expertise.

Types of Aircraft Mechanics

Some mechanics choose to specialize in the area of preventive maintenance, meaning they perform regularly scheduled inspections of aircraft and make repairs as needed. They do not have to perform emergency repairs. Preventive maintenance specialists inspect the engines, landing gear, pressurization systems, brakes, valves, pumps, air conditioning system, and other parts of an aircraft. The inspections occur at

A preventive maintenance mechanic performs an engine overhaul.

regular intervals based on the number of hours a plane has flown and the number of days it has been in operation since its last inspection. Richmond aircraft mechanic Mike Keeling describes why he finds preventive maintenance so attractive: "What appeals to me most . . . is you're not just doing one thing. One minute you're working on an electrical problem, the next minute, it's hydraulics."[34]

The mechanics use precision instruments to measure the wear and tear on different parts. They also utilize X-ray and magnetic equipment to find cracks in the aircraft's fuselage (central body portion), wings, tail, or other parts. They also look for signs of corrosion or distortion in any part of the plane. Anything worn or damaged is replaced or fixed. Parts of the forty-two different systems on a plane, including hydraulic, electrical, mechanical, and structural, are replaced after a certain number of years and hours in operation, even if they do not appear to be worn. This practice minimizes the risk of a part's failure in a system—a failure that could potentially cause an accident—before it occurs. Finally, the preventive maintenance specialist tests the plane to ensure that everything is operating properly.

Other mechanics specialize in doing only emergency repair work. Most of the time a repair specialist responds to a pilot's report of a problem with a plane. For example, while doing the preflight check the pilot may discover the landing gear is not operating properly, the air conditioning system is not functioning at all, or there seems to be fuel leaking from one of the engines. Whatever the

A plane lowers its landing gear, one of the many mechanical systems that may need to be fixed by repair specialists.

Are Aircraft Mechanics Doing Their Jobs?

When a plane crashes, the first thing everyone wants to learn is why. Sometimes an accident can be attributed to pilot error by analyzing data from the voice recorder—the so-called black box—that catches everything said in the cockpit. But if the cause was mechanical breakdown, if an engine failed or the controls lost power, the FAA and the airline will investigate the maintenance record of the airplane.

Controversy surrounds the issue of whether more planes are crashing due to maintenance problems. Pilots complain that their planes are less airworthy than they were before deregulation of the airline industry during the 1980s. With deregulation, competition between airlines became tougher, and airline companies battled to have the most planes flying in the tightest possible schedule. To further save money, airlines employed fewer mechanics, as Captain X in his book *Unfriendly Skies* explains: "It certainly is true that when you land at an airport nowadays you'll be sharing one mechanic, whereas you used to have several assigned to you." Thus, some overworked mechanics, under pressure from the airlines to get the plane back in service as fast as possible, may resort to shortcuts or miss a problem because of haste. Brian Finnegan, president of the Professional Aviation Maintenance Association, blames workplace fatigue and staff shortages for the problem. Finnegan is lobbying for federal protection of mechanics to shield them from being singled out for blame in the event of an accident.

problem, the repair specialist must work quickly to find its cause and fix it so the plane can get back on schedule for its flight. For example, the pilot of a 747 noted that the plane's fuel gauge was not registering properly, so she reported the problem to the repair mechanic on duty at the airport. The repair mechanic immediately tested the electrical system with troubleshooting equipment that would indicate broken or shorted wires. After he found the culprit—a corroded wire that was shorting out—he replaced the defective wire, retested the electrical system, and checked the fuel gauge to make sure the problem was fixed.

Some aircraft mechanics are qualified to work on many different types of planes and are called multicraft mechanics. Multicraft mechanics know how to inspect and repair anything from jumbo jets to small propeller-driven planes and even helicopters. Multicraft mechanics are valuable to airline companies and airports where many different types of aircraft fly in and out because their skills eliminate the need to hire different mechanics for each type of aircraft.

However, many mechanics prefer to specialize in just one type of plane. Some mechanics become experts on jumbo jets and work for major airlines in big airports, but others might focus on smaller propeller planes and work at small municipal airports or local repair shops where private pilots bring their planes for maintenance.

Specializations

Some mechanics get even more specific and become experts in just one section of a plane. There are three areas of specialization for sections: power plant, airframe, and avionics. Power plant specialists work primarily with engines and propellers. Traynor, who, as an engine overhaul mechanic, is a type of power plant specialist, describes a typical day at work:

> Today, for example, we . . . began removal of the L.P.C. (low-pressure compressor) out of . . . a Canadian Airlines 737. The engine was taken from service because it wasn't making power. Borescope (a borescope basically is a probe . . . with a video camera on the end used to view components otherwise inaccessible when the engine is assembled) and test cell analysis . . . revealed [obstructions] in the compressor from a bird strike (birds sucked into the engine). Once the compressor was out, we began disassembling and inspecting. Inspection consists of determining if a component . . . is either serviceable/airworthy, unserviceable/repairable, or unserviceable/scrap.[35]

Airframe specialists may work on any part of the plane with the exception of instruments (navigational devices), power plants (engines), and propellers. Most mechanics, however, are authorized to perform both types of specialties and are called A & P (airframe and power plant) mechanics.

Avionics technicians maintain and repair the navigational instruments, radio communications systems, weather radar systems, and computers that control flight, engines, and other electronic functions on the plane. Avionics specialist Suzie Ashburne says, "I like doing the modifications on aircraft, which is when you run all the new wires and systems, and change all the components. There have been about 83 modifications on the aircraft I am working on at the moment, and some of them have been really big—like putting in a new video system."[36]

Licensing and Training

Most specialists have earned one or more mechanic's licenses from the FAA. Although a license is not required for a mechanic to work on an aircraft as long as a licensed mechanic supervises, most employers prefer to hire licensed mechanics. Major airlines, the biggest employer of aircraft mechanics, usually require mechanics to have at least a high school diploma and an FAA mechanic's license with an A & P rating. Traynor explains that "engines and all their parts are too expensive for someone with no previous experience to be handling, and besides, it would cost too much money for a company to train someone from the ground up. So you really need the course [certificate program to prepare for license exam] to get a job."[37]

To earn any type of FAA license, aircraft mechanics must either have documented work experience or have completed a course of study at an institution with an FAA-approved program. Mechanics

A student mechanic participates in a hands-on examination of an airplane's engine, a test required by the FAA.

must have a minimum of eighteen months of experience to qualify for a mechanic's license with a rating in power plants, airframe, or avionics. An A & P license requires a mechanic to have worked at least thirty months with both airframes and engines.

Most aircraft mechanics learn their trade and get the experience needed to earn a license by enrolling in and completing a college or trade school program. According to Harold L. O'Brien, an aircraft mechanic and avionics chief at Dryden Flight Research Center, "If someone wishes to make a career in aeronautics they should have a real strong background in mathematics, chemistry, and physics to enter an engineering program. If their desire is to be an aircraft mechanic, electrician or technician they still should have some basic knowledge in those areas."[38] Prospective aircraft mechanics may choose from about two hundred mechanic schools with FAA-approved programs in avionics, power plants, and airframes. About a third of these schools also offer students the opportunity to go beyond the certificate program and earn two- or four-year degrees in avionics, aviation technology, or aviation maintenance management.

FAA-approved mechanic school certificate programs require at least nineteen hundred hours of class time. Usually students take two to two and a half years to complete a program, in which they learn not only the principles and applications of aircraft technology but also how to properly use the tools and equipment of the trade to diagnose, inspect, and repair. Often the initial coursework involves mathematics, physics, chemistry, computer science, general electronics, and mechanical drawing, because knowledge of these disciplines is important to understanding how aircraft technology works and how it can be repaired. As computers increasingly control aircraft, programs are emphasizing aviation electronics. Students learn how turbine engines (used on large jets) and piston engines (used on smaller planes) work; how composite materials such as graphite, fiberglass, and boron are used in aircraft; and how these materials react to the stress imposed on them during high-speed and high-altitude flight.

Once the course of study has been completed, students must then pass written and oral tests given by the FAA. They must also pass a hands-on examination that requires them to demonstrate that they can do the work. Even after the certificate is earned, mechanics must demonstrate they possess up-to-date technical knowledge and appropriate skills in order to keep their licenses. The FAA requires mechan-

Mechanics work on a jet's engine. Two-thirds of aircraft mechanics work for airlines or airports.

ics to have either one thousand hours of work experience within a two-year period or to take a sixteen-hour training course that upgrades their skills and knowledge or refreshes what they have previously learned. However, in order to keep up with the furious pace with which increasingly complex aircraft designs are appearing, most mechanics continually receive training through their employers.

The Ups and Downs of Being an Aircraft Mechanic

Generally, about two-thirds of aircraft mechanics are employed by airlines or airports. Only one out of eight work for the federal government (FAA and military), and about one out of seven work for aircraft assembly companies. The remainder are employed by independent repair shops or companies that own planes to transport their executives and clients.

Regardless of their employer, most mechanics work inside hangars, which are covered and enclosed structures designed for housing airplanes. Nevertheless, there are times when mechanics must work outdoors—even when the weather is freezing or wet and it is the middle of the night—to make repairs quickly and get the plane back into service as soon as possible. This is most likely to happen when a plane that is scheduled for takeoff suddenly is delayed because the pilot discovered a last-minute problem during the preflight check, as the experience of this aircraft mechanic demonstrates:

The Beech 1900 commuter aircraft was parked at the far side of the ramp with the left engine cowling opened. On top of a metal work stand, a lone figure, his back hunched in an attempt to shield his hands from the cold wind, was working to change the PT-6 igniter box. Replacing the igniter box is usually an easy repair. One which the aircraft mechanic now working on the engine must have changed many times before. But today the job was made difficult, more time consuming, by the cold wind and stiff fingers. Fingers that sometimes stuck painfully to the cold soaked metal of the engine's turbine housing.[39]

In the interest of time, mechanics are often called out to diagnose and fix the problem at the terminal gate rather than taking the time to taxi the plane out to a hangar and then back again when it is ready for service. Mark Ebben, a Northwest Airlines mechanic, told the *Detroit News* that his job was sometimes "more like working on a racing car pit crew, with members forced to solve mechanical problems as quickly as possible."[40]

During such times, mechanics are under a great deal of pressure to make repairs as fast as possible without compromising safety. Although they need to make certain the repairs are done properly, haste is sometimes necessary so that flight schedules can be maintained and passengers are not inconvenienced by long delays. The pressure to work fast while keeping in mind that the lives of hundreds of people depend on your work can be very stressful to aircraft mechanics, as Adam Traynor explains:

> Once I sign my name saying a particular part is airworthy, my signature becomes legal. When I say a part is airworthy, I'm saying that this part can be trusted to carry 200 plus people 35,000 feet in the sky. . . . So if that one single blade that I deemed to be airworthy during my inspection comes loose during takeoff or during cruise—catastrophic failure is inevitable.[41]

Sometimes, however, flight schedules are disrupted no matter how skilled the mechanic is. Some problems simply cannot be repaired in a matter of minutes, and unexpected delays that are beyond the mechanic's control can happen. A mechanic at Northwest Airlines found a tiny leak in a stainless steel fuel line during a routine preflight check. As the passengers boarded the jet the mechanic prepared to fix the leak quickly and allow the plane leave on schedule. Unfortunately, the mechanic discovered the airport did not have the part he needed to fix the leak. The part would have to be ordered, and there would be at least a day's wait for it to arrive. The passengers had to leave the plane and wait three hours for a different flight that was headed to their destination.

The Anatomy of an Airplane

There are three basic parts to the structure, or airframe, of a plane: the fuselage, the wings, and the tail surfaces. The fuselage consists of the main body of the plane, which houses the cockpit, passenger cabin, and cargo compartment. Attached to the sides of the fuselage are the wings, the lift-creating parts of the plane. Each wing has metal flaps on it that move. If the flaps on the left wing are up, the plane turns to the right, and if those on the right wing are up, the plane turns to the left. The tail surfaces are attached to the rear of the fuselage and add stability to the plane's movements.

The parts of the plane that are not of the airframe are the propulsion system, landing gear, and instruments. The propulsion system is what powers the plane, giving it the speed needed to create enough air pressure to lift the wings. Small planes may be powered by an engine and a propeller, a rotating unit of two to four planks centrally connected that create thrust under the plane. Large jets do not use propellers; instead, they rely on several turbine engines that power the plane by rapidly expanding gases. Turbine engines allow jets to fly at faster speeds than other types of engines or propellers do.

The landing gear consists of struts, wheels, and brakes used while taking off or landing on a runway. In many small planes the gear is permanently fixed to the bottom of the fuselage, but on large jets it is retracted into the fuselage to prevent a drag effect that can slow down the plane.

The instruments, most of which are located in the cockpit, allow the pilot to control the plane's speed and direction, navigate along a flight path, and communicate with air traffic control.

Recently, because airlines have had to tighten their budgets due to rising fuel costs, mechanics have claimed that some airlines push them to take unsafe shortcuts in order to keep planes flying because delayed flights mean lost revenue for the airlines. Mechanics have spoken out against such practices and have come under fire from their employers for doing so. For example, in March 2000 sixty-four mechanics of Alaska Airlines wrote a letter to their company's top management complaining about safety violations by the airline company's maintenance management in Seattle, Washington. Rather than conduct an investigation to find out if the accusations were true, Alaska Airlines simply tried to stop the mechanics from speaking out. The mechanics, whose concerns were supported by Alaska Airlines pilots who complained of maintenance problems with planes, were intimidated during meetings with the company's top officials.

In addition to stress due to heavy responsibility and the challenge of balancing efficiency with safety, mechanics are also subject to physical risks in their everyday work. They must often lift or pull objects that weigh up to seventy pounds, resulting in back problems. Mechanics frequently stand, sit, kneel, or lie in awkward positions to get to hard-to-reach sections of a plane, such as the wings or fuselage, sometimes high up on scaffolds or ladders. Although such accidents are not common, mechanics do run the risk of falling from

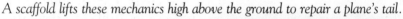

A scaffold lifts these mechanics high above the ground to repair a plane's tail.

Airplane mechanics, like these working on a jet's interior, make an average salary of fourteen to eighteen dollars per hour.

these precarious places. In addition, the extreme noise and vibrations that mechanics are exposed to when operating or testing certain parts or equipment may result in hearing damage.

Despite the risks involved, most aircraft mechanics love their jobs because of the challenges offered them in problem solving while utilizing technical skills. Many mechanics are thrilled to have the opportunity to work on high-tech aircraft, especially the jets that are big and fast. Mechanics are also attracted to their profession by the potential to make good money, although during the 1990s wage increases did not always keep up with those in other airline industry professions.

Mechanics who work for the major airlines earn the highest wages, averaging over twenty dollars per hour, but those with experience may earn as much as thirty dollars per hour. Most mechanics start out at a modest hourly wage of fourteen dollars and advance to an average of eighteen dollars an hour. Aircraft mechanics can increase their pay with advancements from experience or further training. Budget cuts by the airline industry have curtailed higher wages for many mechanics, prompting young people who would otherwise be interested in the profession to enter other types of technical careers, such as computers, that pay much higher.

With fewer people entering the mechanic profession during the 1990s—a decade when plane ticket prices decreased and the numbers of people flying grew—there is a shortage of aircraft mechanics compared to the numbers of planes being flown by airlines. Currently 137,000 mechanics work in the airline industry, but the federal government estimates there is a need for 12,000 to 18,000 more. Gerald Koenig, chief executive officer of Evergreen Air Center near Tucson, Arizona, said one effect of the shortage is "the price of this talent [mechanics] is increasing. So flying public . . . the airplane's going to be as safe as it always was, but you're going to get the shock at the ticket counter when you pay."[42] Other airline industry professionals contend that the shortage can also be alleviated by scheduling fewer flights or by simply accepting that some delays due to maintenance issues are unavoidable to ensure safety.

Opportunities for Advancement

Aircraft mechanics who stay with their profession may, with many years of experience, advance to lead mechanic or crew chief, responsible for supervising mechanics of less experience. Likewise, those who work in repair shops may become shop supervisors. Those who hold an inspector's authorization, which can be earned after holding an A & P license for three years and passing an FAA exam, have the best chance of gaining supervisor positions. Supervisors who pass employer-based examinations may be promoted to executive positions in which they manage the maintenance department or perform administrative duties such as tracking parts inventories or overseeing repair budgets.

Whatever their level of advancement, all aircraft mechanics share the awesome responsibility of keeping multimillion-dollar vehicles in safe working order. As Traynor says:

> Aircraft maintenance as well as engine overhaul are pursuits which require much patience and a commitment to the highest standards. . . . As . . . airline pilots know, you can't exactly pull over to the side of the road 30,000 feet over the Atlantic [Ocean] after an engine failure—the only thing you can do is look at each other. Having said this, you can see that it takes a special kind of person to work in aviation.[43]

Chapter 5

Astronauts

Perhaps few occupations in modern times have conveyed such a sense of mystery, adventure, and bravery as that of the astronaut, that amazing space traveler. In fact, the word *astronaut* comes from Greek words that mean "star sailor," which, in a way, is exactly what these professionals do—sail through space on a voyage of great discovery.

Although it sounds exciting, being an astronaut is not for everybody. Astronauts come from all walks of life, but what they have in common is a fierce dedication to science and learning. Astronauts are scientists and sometimes pilots specially trained by the National Aeronautics and Space Administration (NASA), an agency of the federal government, in research methods, spacecraft operation, and how to live in space. Astronauts thrive on adventure and love challenging, even dangerous, activities.

How Does Someone Become an Astronaut?

Many people think that it takes specialized education and years of work experience to become an astronaut. Surprisingly, however, becoming an astronaut takes no longer than the average time it takes most people to complete graduate and postgraduate studies to enter other careers. Astronaut Charlie Bolden says, "Start with the basics and get them down first. . . . You can't do anything without math and science."[44]

NASA has very high standards in choosing its astronaut candidates. Basically, a person must have at least a bachelor's degree in engineering, biological sciences, physical sciences, or mathematics. In addition, a person must have a minimum of three years of work experience related to the degree, in which increasingly greater responsibility has been taken on. Astronaut Ellen Ochoa says, "There isn't one particular type of work experience that NASA is looking for. NASA—like any other employer—wants to know how well a person has done. If you come from a research background, they'd look

An astronaut stands in the space shuttle cargo bay. NASA chooses only the best-trained and educated people for its astronaut positions.

at published work in technical journals, lecturing . . . experience, and also any awards that you may have won."[45] Those who want to pilot spacecraft must meet the additional requirement of over one thousand hours of experience as a pilot in command of a jet.

Anyone who meets the basic requirements may apply for an astronaut position, but NASA is extremely selective about whom it chooses. Every other year NASA accepts applications, and from the thousands it receives, only about one hundred are chosen to undergo the screening process.

Once chosen for screening, an applicant must travel to Johnson Space Center in Houston, Texas, for a weeklong session of interviews and examinations. During this week the Astronaut Selection Board (ASB) again reviews each applicant's recommendations, looking for testimonials that suggest superior problem-solving abilities, communication skills, and teamwork characteristics. The ASB also interviews each applicant, as former astronaut Mike Mullane explains:

> When I was interviewed . . . I was never asked any technical questions. . . . What NASA wants to know is what type of a

"person" you are. They are looking for well rounded, outgoing, team-oriented people to be astronauts. So they typically ask general "life" questions. "What are your hobbies? What jobs have you had? . . . What have you found most rewarding? Most challenging? What do you feel is your greatest accomplishment?" . . . Sure NASA wants very smart people, but they want those smart people to be team "players," to have demonstrated an ability to work with others, to be people with varied life experiences.[46]

Applicants who lack the necessary interpersonal and psychological attributes are rejected.

Although the process may seem harsh, it is important for NASA to choose only applicants who demonstrate the highest standards because flying in space carries risks and there is little or no margin for error. An astronaut without good communication skills might cause a misunderstanding between crew members, leading to a grave mistake that results in damage to the spacecraft or injury to a crew member.

In addition, all applicants are examined for medical and physical problems, and those without the required bill of good health are also dismissed. It is imperative that astronauts be free from medical problems because of the effect microgravity has on the body. Microgravity is the condition very close to zero gravity or weightlessness, in which astronauts must work. *National Geographic* writer Michael E. Long explains how microgravity affects humans:

> Deprived of gravity . . . body fluids surge to chest and head. Neck veins bulge. Faces puff. The heart enlarges a bit, as do other organs. Sensing too much fluid, the body begins to excrete it. . . . The production of red blood cells decreases, rendering astronauts slightly anemic. With the loss of fluid, legs shrink. Spinal discs expand, and so does the astronaut—a six-footer can soon measure six-foot-two and suffer a backache.[47]

As a result, people with heart disease, circulation problems, spinal abnormalities, and many other conditions cannot safely live in space.

Astronaut Training

After all of the evaluations are completed, the ASB selects twenty candidates from the pool of applicants to begin an intensive two-year training program. Candidates are not actually astronauts until

All About Space Suits

Space suits are actually small self-contained spacecraft designed to keep the wearer healthy when working outside of the main spacecraft. The space suit is made of twelve layers, each of which serve a different purpose. The first two layers are made from Spandex and have plastic tubes sewn in to hold coolant. The next two layers are made of nylon and Dracon, followed by seven layers of thermal materials. The exterior layer is made of Gortex and Kevlar, a bullet-proof material used for protection against small meteoroids.

While in a space suit, an astronaut is supplied oxygen for breathing and an appropriate level of pressure is maintained to keep body fluids in a liquid state—without the pressure, fluids would boil over and explode the body. In addition, a constant temperature is maintained because of temperature extremes that occur in space without the protection of the earth's atmosphere. Otherwise, the side of the astronaut facing the sun would burn up in sunlight 250 degrees Fahrenheit while the side facing deep space would freeze at -250 degrees. A microphone and headphones for two-way communications with the main spacecraft are also provided.

To move around in space, the suit is equipped with a manned maneuvering unit (MMU)—that is, a backpack with nitrogen jets that propel the astronaut. The astronaut can control the direction of movement by using hand instruments that direct the jets. Astronauts wear MMUs when they need to move around in space to deploy, repair, or retrieve satellites or part of the exterior of the spacecraft.

A space suit is incredibly heavy, weighing about three hundred pounds. Fortunately, in space microgravity makes the suit weigh much less than it does on Earth. The bulk can still make working in a space suit strenuous, but astronauts can last about five to seven hours before endurance as well as oxygen, water, and other vital necessities are depleted.

they complete the training. During the training period candidates study math, astronomy, physics, geology, meteorology, and oceanography through NASA-based courses. They also gain an understanding of the technology used in spaceflight, including navigational tools, orbital mechanics, and materials processing—that is, what materials spacecraft are made of and the techniques used to create the materials. Candidates become familiar with every part of a space shuttle and its systems. Lieutenant Colonel Catherine G. Coleman, who was chosen as an astronaut candidate in 1992, explains how her experience grew in training: "I needed to learn safety procedures, how the space shuttle works, how the space station operates, software information and what to do if things go wrong. Basically, I needed to learn how to be a space shuttle operator."[48]

Beyond such core knowledge, astronaut candidates learn survival strategies and everyday living techniques for space. By using scuba gear, they can simulate a weightless environment in water. In addition, they learn how to do everything from eating to repairing a wire in NASA's microgravity chamber. Candidates learn how to keep the shuttle maintained. They are also trained to work in both

Clouds of smoke billow from a space shuttle launch. Astronaut candidates must become familiar with all of a space shuttle's systems.

low- and high-pressure environments and how to perform tasks while wearing a bulky space suit. Maintaining physical fitness is important; at the end of the training, candidates must pass a swimming test that requires them to swim the length of a twenty-five-meter pool three times while wearing a flight suit and tennis shoes.

Candidates training to be spacecraft pilots must fulfill additional requirements. Since the controls on a T-38 jet are identical to those of the space shuttle, pilot candidates spend at least fifteen hours each month flying jets.

Jets are also used to train all candidates in aircraft safety, and they receive training in ejection, parachute use, and survival. These skills are important in the event the jet or shuttle, after reentering the earth's atmosphere, becomes disabled and they must eject or make an emergency landing.

Beginning the Astronaut Career

Once the two-year training has been completed, candidates officially become astronauts employed by NASA. However, all new astronauts must wait at least one year before they may be selected for a mission on board a spacecraft. During this year, astronauts continue their extensive training, becoming familiar with all of the individual space shuttle systems and using simulators to practice launching, orbiting, entry into the earth's atmosphere, and landing. Some astronauts also learn to use the robotic arm on the space shuttle to manipulate cargo.

Those astronauts who are trained to use the shuttle's robotic arm will have special duties when they are selected for a spaceflight. They are called mission specialists, and as a member of a crew they are responsible for specifically assigned shuttle operation duties: doing space walks when necessary for research or repair tasks and conducting scientific experiments. Coleman served as a mission specialist on her first space shuttle mission, assisting with several experiments in the pressurized Spacelab module on the shuttle. "I personally interacted with 30 experiments, many of which were in fluid physics and crystal growth," said Coleman. "This is where my training as a scientist really came in handy, as it is a challenge to work quickly but well. It is like having 30 customers in 16 days. There isn't time for mistakes. You need to go up there and do your best."[49]

Several mission specialists have spent extended periods living and working in space. Shannon Lucid served as a mission specialist for 188 days on the Russian space station Mir, where she helped with

A shuttle's robotic arm lifts a satellite from the shuttle cargo bay. Only mission specialists are trained for this duty.

experiments in growing different types of agricultural plants. In fact, as the American record holder for length of time in space, Lucid was herself an experimental subject. During her stay and after her return to Earth, researchers evaluated the effects of long-term exposure to microgravity on her health and fitness.

Every crew includes several mission specialists who are led by a commander, and the pilot, who is second in command. In charge of the mission, the commander supervises the crew and oversees operations of the space shuttle. Although the pilot may also serve as the commander, the major responsibility of this position is to operate the spacecraft and to deploy satellites or other payloads.

The payload is the material carried by the spacecraft either for the craft's operation or for conducting experiments. The payload is sponsored by a government agency or a private company or institution that is helping to fund the mission. For example, if scientists at a university want to experiment with growing edible plants in space, the university might pay for some of the costs of a mission on which such experiments will be performed, including the cost of seeds, plants, fertilizer, chemicals, and other materials or tools required.

Working on a Space Mission

Once an astronaut has been selected for a mission, preparation begins ten months before the launch date. Intense training during the preparation period allows the crew members to get used to working together as a team. As they hone their cooperative skills, the team performs regular flight operations in simulation according to the projected flight schedule. This is crucial because crew members who bicker among themselves may soon be arguing with mission control on Earth, thereby threatening the success of the mission. Great attention is given to training in every type of emergency situation imaginable, including engine failure, electrical problems, damage to the shuttle, and injuries or illness among the crew.

On the day of the launch, the crew assembles at the launch pad at Cape Canaveral in Florida. From here, they climb up into the shuttle's crew cabin, the hatch is closed behind them, and they buckle into their seats, lying on their backs with their feet up because of the shuttle's upright position on the pad. Then they wait as the countdown proceeds. One astronaut describes what the launch is like:

The Shuttle sways forward and backwards once, by about 5 feet . . . shaking and vibrating strongly. But the crew hears nothing of the thunderous noise generated by the engines. Then the count reaches zero, and the voice in your helmet radio calls "SRB Ignition—Lift-Off!" The two strapped-on solid rocket boosters ignite, and the Shuttle starts to move upward. You don't feel much acceleration at this time, no more than in an airplane during takeoff. The solid boosters do not burn smoothly at all; their thrusting feels rough and bumpy. The crew cabin shakes and rattles . . . like a car driving at top speed over cobblestones. . . . At two minutes after liftoff . . . things become quiet and smooth, and every crewmember feels tremendous relief. . . . At 7-1/2 minutes into the flight . . . the force pressing you down has grown to . . . three times earth's gravity. . . . Breathing has become hard enough for you to choose consciously between going without breathing (and suffocating) or forcing yourself to inhale and each time lift your chest with the heavy suit on top. . . . And finally, there's "MECO" (main engines cut-off). Within seconds, the thrust from the engines drops off to zero; just as suddenly the pressure disappears from your chest, and you become weightless. You are in space![50]

Once in space, the astronauts begin their mission duties according to the role that NASA has assigned each crew member. Because each mission is different, an astronaut who serves on two or more missions will not have the same duties or play the same role each time. For example, mission specialist Rhea Seddon, one of the first six female astronauts in the United States, played different roles in two Spacelab Life Sciences missions, one in 1991 (SLS-1) and one

The Space Shuttle at a Glance

Since its first mission in 1981, the space shuttle has flown over six hundred astronauts and 3 million pounds of payload cargo into space. The shuttle is a reusable spacecraft and is unique because it can carry satellites to and from the earth's orbit. The entire unit consists of three parts: the orbiter, which houses the crew; the external fuel tank, which burns up after use in the earth's atmosphere; and two rocket boosters, which help propel the shuttle upward and are dropped off after two minutes, to be retrieved and later reused during another launch. The shuttle, which has a wingspan of just over 78 feet, is launched like a rocket and orbits the earth at a speed of 17,440 miles per hour, but it lands just like an airplane.

The shuttle orbits within a range of 115 to 400 miles above the earth's surface. The four orbiters currently in use—*Columbia* (the first shuttle), *Atlantis*, *Discovery*, and *Endeavor*—have collectively flown about a hundred missions. This is only a quarter of their projected lifespan since each shuttle individually is designed to make one hundred trips into orbit.

Over the last twenty years the shuttle has undergone many changes. Structural and operational improvements have decreased flight problems by 70 percent, making the shuttle safer to fly. Today the shuttle can carry eight tons more cargo than it could during the early 1980s. As a result of improvements in safety and efficiency, the cost of operating the shuttle has decreased by 40 percent since 1990. NASA plans to continue using the shuttle for at least another decade to deploy payload satellites and to provide transportation between Earth and the International Space Station.

in 1993 (SLS-2). In SLS-1 Seddon was responsible for experimenting with the care, housing, and behavior of animals in space. She even let a rat float in the workstation to see how it reacted to weightlessness. "This helped to answer some questions about animal handling that were very important for the future of life sciences research," Seddon explained. "I think if we hadn't done that we would have had to develop all kinds of procedures to deal with the possibility that the animals might be aggressive. . . . That's certainly one of the things we like to do on each mission, to help future missions predict or prepare for what they are going to do."[51]

However, on the next mission, SLS-2, Seddon served as the payload commander and was responsible for overseeing experiments in animal dissection in space. The experiments were designed to assess what problems there might be in using the equipment, animal handling, and surgery procedures in a weightless environment. As a payload commander, Seddon described the unique challenge of her role in SLS-2 as "blending the needs, desires, wishes, and priorities of engineers and managers from NASA, the crew from NASA, and the outside scientists."[52]

Living in Space

Besides conducting experiments and operating the space shuttle, astronauts must deal with the challenges of living in microgravity while in space. Weightlessness can make everyday activities like eating and sleeping difficult. When astronauts sleep they must squeeze into small bunks that can be covered to keep out the noise in the rest of the shuttle. One astronaut describes this as

> somewhat disconcerting to find oneself inside a narrow shoebox, but with most astronauts it takes only 10–15 seconds to suddenly feel the illusion that you're comfortable and on your back. . . . You need to get used to the lack of touch on your back or on your side, because you are really floating in your [sleeping] bag, only lightly touched by the ties holding you down.[53]

Eating in space also presents the problem of how to keep food and utensils from floating away. Knives, forks, and spoons stay on a tray through the use of a magnet, and astronauts keep the tray tied to their lap to hold it in place. Some foods, like peas or beans, are prepared in a sauce so they will stick to the spoon or fork and not float off. Beverages can be drunk from a squeeze bottle similar to sports water bottles. Most meals are freeze-dried and must be reconstituted with water. Because of the fluid changes that microgravity causes in the human body, the senses of taste and smell are diminished. As a result, most astronauts like to season their food a lot to make it more flavorful.

Serving as a crew member on the space shuttle is not all work, however. All astronauts are scheduled recreation time when they are free to do whatever they want. Some astronauts pass their leisure time reading, listening to music, chatting with crew members, or playing games. Others use laptops to write e-mails to family and friends or talk to people on Earth through a ham radio. Many astronauts say their favorite leisure activity is gazing out the shuttle windows into space and watching Earth.

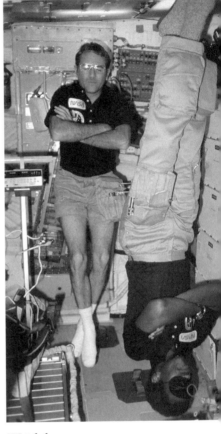

Weightless astronauts rest aboard a space shuttle.

Coming Home

When the mission nears its end, after a stay of anywhere from five to fifteen days in space, the astronauts once again gather in the crew cabin to prepare for reentering the earth's atmosphere and landing. Most of the reentry, which takes about thirty minutes, is controlled by the autopilot of the shuttle rather than the mission pilot because a human error could cause the shuttle to burn up in the atmosphere. To start the reentry process, the pilot turns the shuttle so that its tail end is facing the earth and then fires the small engines located at the rear. The firing of the engines actually brakes the shuttle from its orbit of twenty-eight thousand kilometers per hour and slows it down so much that the shuttle is pulled toward Earth by gravity. During this period the shuttle slowly turns until it is facing Earth. As the shuttle proceeds through the atmosphere, thick tiles on its exterior protect it from the extreme heat resulting from friction with the air. The closer the shuttle gets to the ground, the more the air slows down its descent. Only during the last couple of minutes before landing does the pilot take over the shuttle's controls, steering it like a jet toward the runway at Edwards Air Force Base in California's Mojave Desert, where it comes down on landing gear just like an airplane.

After the shuttle comes to a stop, the astronauts exit and report to NASA officials and payload-sponsor representatives for meetings, called debriefings, where they discuss the successes and problems encountered during the mission and undergo medical examinations. Once the debriefings are finished, astronauts move on to other responsibilities, which may include beginning preparations for another mission, helping other astronauts develop experiments, or doing follow-up research based on the discoveries of prior missions. Most astronauts serve on an average of three shuttle missions, but with the development of the International Space Station (ISS), many are aiming to serve for extended periods doing research at a more leisurely pace on the ISS.

A shuttle pilot like this one must take over the controls during the last few minutes before landing.

An Astronaut's Career

After many years of training and serving on missions, some astronauts move on to other types of positions within NASA, although many astronauts also retire from NASA, opting to advance their careers through research at public or private universities, companies, or other organizations. All astronauts are committed to staying with NASA at least five years after they serve on a mission, but many have worked there for twenty years. Career astronauts may advance to NASA management, and others help train new astronauts or assist crews with preparations for a mission. Others, such as Coleman, aim to work in mission control, the group of people responsible for communicating with and directing astronauts from Earth. Coleman says she wants to work in mission control because

> I think it will be very helpful that I know from experience how busy the astronauts are. There needs to be a balance between communication and knowing that they are up there doing their jobs. For instance, I can help make the decisions about whether it is important to discuss with them their plans for the next four hours or to just give them a few more minutes to complete the tasks they are currently doing.[54]

Regardless of what capacity they work in for NASA, all astronauts are considered civil service employees, and their salaries are based on the standard federal government pay scale. Many people assume that because of the risks astronauts take when they fly into space that they are paid grandiose salaries. However, according to the pay scale, new astronauts earn about $39,000 annually while the most experienced may earn as much as $78,000 per year.

A Risky Business

The modest salary relative to the job responsibilities does not disturb most astronauts—after all, they are in the job for the love of science and the thrill of adventure, not to get rich. Nevertheless, astronauts do have some complaints about their work. Perhaps the most common complaint is the amount of time they spend working, which sometimes can last from 7:30 in the morning until 11:00 at night. Bolden says, "When you have a spouse and you don't see the Sun on them . . . that gets tired pretty fast."[55]

Surprisingly, most astronauts do not complain about the risks related to their job—and neither do their families. Both astronauts

Space shuttle Challenger *explodes in 1986. Accidents during the launch or re-entry are a risk for astronauts aboard a space shuttle.*

and their family members learn to cope emotionally with the physical risks. Ochoa explains, "We train for all different kinds of scenarios—most of which aren't very good. When you have a pretty good idea of what you should be doing in an emergency, it tends to reduce those emotions."[56]

This, of course, does not mean that astronauts simply ignore the risks: They are well aware of the precarious situation they put themselves in every time they go into space, as Mullane explains:

The risks of flying the space shuttle are not insignificant. As I write this, there have been 74 successful shuttle flights since *Challenger* [exploded right after launch in 1986]. I worry this success might have lulled some people into thinking the shuttle is as safe and as reliable as an airliner. It's not.

. . . I'm not saying this to discourage anybody from applying to be an astronaut, but just do so as an informed person as to the risks involved. In just 8 ¹/₂ minutes, the space shuttle will convert 4 million pounds of propellant into a speed of near-ly 5 miles per second and an altitude of about 200 miles

The Future of Medical Care in Space

The following excerpt is from Michael E. Long's article "Surviving in Space," which appeared in the January 2001 issue of National Geographic. *It details how medical care would take place on an extend-ed journey through space, such as a trip to and from Mars, which could take as long as six years. Many of these plans currently are being devel-oped at the National Space Biomedical Research Institute (NSBRI).*

To cope with infection [Jeffrey] Sutton [NSBRI research team leader] plans a factory to make drugs, even new ones, to cope with possible organisms on Mars. Miniaturized optical and ultrasound devices will image body and brain—perhaps pinpointing the cause of a headache—while a small x-ray machine keeps track of any bone loss. . . . The crew will be able to craft body parts . . . tooled to an astronaut's personal anatomy and genome [genetic code] stored in computer memory.

Excuse me, body parts?

Yes, says Sutton, researchers are building artificial liver, bone, and cartilage tissue right now. "Let's take two worst cases: An astro-naut bangs into a piece of equipment and suffers a . . . blood clot on the brain, and also severs part of an ear. On Earth that's a heli-copter flight to special treatment at a trauma center."

In sick bay on Sutton's spacecraft, an astronaut . . . will [use] the optical imaging system to locate the clot with a laser, then dissipate it with a tightly focused beam. To deal with the ear, he consults a three-dimensional computer model of the injured person's body. The com-puter teaches him how to build a . . . model of the ear, then to grow new cartilage containing the astronaut's DNA [genetic material]. "[Next] you just align part A with part B," says Sutton. "Then an ultrasound pulse heats and seals the wound."

[above ground level]. In other words, a shuttle launch is a controlled explosion. It will NEVER be routine. It will always carry some significant dangers.[57]

In addition to the risks of being blown up during the launch and burning up during the reentry to the atmosphere, simply being in space carries its own risks. Because astronauts do not have the earth's atmosphere to shield them from the sun's rays, they are exposed to harmful radiation. Almost every astronaut returns from space suffering from bone loss, disorientation, and weight loss. Much research is being done to find ways of combating these problems, but until scientists solve them, the possibility of long-term space travel remains unlikely.

Nevertheless, NASA hopes to someday send astronauts to other planets in our solar system, particularly Mars. A trip to Mars would take three years one way, and then the crew would have to spend at least a year on the surface of the planet conducting various research projects before making the long return trip home to Earth. The ISS will help NASA personnel plan a Mars expedition by giving astronauts the opportunity to experiment with long-term human survival in space.

Until then, there is still plenty for astronauts at NASA to do. There is no end to the training and researching they participate in, and the thrill of adventure when serving on a mission in space is ever present. Most of all, they gain fulfillment from the challenge of constant learning, as Coleman, who was a research chemist before becoming an astronaut, explains: "The biggest challenge about being involved in the space program is the need to be able to be good at and know a lot about a lot of things. It's not just chemistry anymore."[58]

Notes

Introduction: Aeronautics: A Mainstay of Modern Life

1. Quoted in Darcy Frey, "Something's Got to Give," *New York Times*, March 24, 1996. www.airtrafficcafe.com/something_got_to_give.shtml.

Chapter One: Pilots

2. Quoted in John Thorn, ed., *The Armchair Aviator*. New York: Charles Scribner's Sons, 1983, pp. 21–25.

3. Joel Freeman, "How Becoming an Airline Pilot Works," How Stuff Works. www.howstuffworks.com/pilot.htm.

4. Freeman, "How Becoming an Airline Pilot Works."

5. Captain X and Reynolds Dodson, *Unfriendly Skies: Revelations of a Deregulated Airline Pilot*. New York: Doubleday, 1989, p. 36.

6. Quoted in the Editors of *Flying Magazine*, *I Learned About Flying from That!* New York: Delacorte, 1976, p. 60.

7. Captain X and Dodson, *Unfriendly Skies*, pp. 81–85.

8. Captain X and Dodson, *Unfriendly Skies*, p. 27.

9. Quoted in Captain X and Dodson, *Unfriendly Skies*, pp. 167–68.

10. Captain X and Dodson, *Unfriendly Skies*, p. 28.

11. Freeman, "How Becoming an Airline Pilot Works."

Chapter Two: Flight Attendants

12. Wendy Stafford, "The Mystique of the Flight Attendant," Aviation Career.net, August 20, 2001. www.aviationcareer.net/features/ fa_04112001_03.cfm.

13. Stafford, "The Mystique of the Flight Attendant."

14. Quoted in Travel, "The Passenger from Hell," August 17, 1999. www.salon.com/travel/diary/hest/1999/08/17/passenger/html.

15. Quoted in Aviation News Web, "Flight Attendant Reports." www.aviationnewsweb.com/aviation1/flight_attendant_reports.htm.

16. Stafford, "The Mystique of the Flight Attendant."

17. Quoted in World Wide Aviation Employment Assistance Website, "A Flight Attendant Talks About Her Job." www.avjobs.com/ careers/ flightattendant/flightattendanttalks.htm.

18. Captain X and Dodson, *Unfriendly Skies*, p. 159.

19. Captain X and Dodson, *Unfriendly Skies*, p. 156.

20. Quoted in World Wide Aviation Employment Assistance Website, "A Flight Attendant Talks About Her Job."

21. Quoted in World Wide Aviation Employment Assistance Website, "A Flight Attendant Talks About Her Job."

22. Quoted in World Wide Aviation Employment Assistance Website, "A Flight Attendant Talks About Her Job."

Chapter Three: Air Traffic Controllers

23. Paul E. Illman, *The Pilot's Air Traffic Control Handbook*. Blue Ridge Summit, PA: Tab Books, 1989, p. 199.

24. Illman, *The Pilot's Air Traffic Control Handbook*, p. 119.

25. Captain X and Dodson, *Unfriendly Skies*, p. 110.

26. Captain X and Dodson, *Unfriendly Skies*, p. 106.

27. Frey, "Something's Got to Give."

28. Frey, "Something's Got to Give."

29. Frey, "Something's Got to Give."

30. Quoted in Frey, "Something's Got to Give."

31. Quoted in Illman, *The Pilot's Air Traffic Control Handbook*, p. 193.

32. Quoted in Frey, "Something's Got to Give."

Chapter Four: Aircraft Mechanics

33. Adam Traynor, "Aircraft Maintenance," Jet Careers Website. www.jetcareers.com/maintenance.htm.

34. Quoted in Chip Jones, "The Plane Truth: Inside the Hangar with Aircraft Mechanics at Richmond International Airport," *Richmond Times-Dispatch*, August 6, 2001, p. D-14.

35. Traynor, "Aircraft Maintenance."

36. Quoted in KiwiCareers Website, "Avionics Engineering Tradesperson." www.careers.co.nz/jobs/4c_mec/j38363h.htm.

37. Traynor, "Aircraft Maintenance."

38. Harold L. O'Brien, "Interview—Avionics and Instrumentation, Harold L. O'Brien." http://wings.avkids.com/Careers/obrien.html.

39. Bill O'Brien, "Grease Monkey," Aircraft Maintenance. www.qtm.net/~jetdoc/amt.htm.

40. Quoted in Francis X. Donnelly, "Mechanics Want Pay Like Lives Depend on It," *Detroit News*, April 6, 2001.
41. Traynor, "Aircraft Maintenance."
42. Quoted in Ted Robbins, "Wanted: Mechanics," NewsHour with Jim Lehrer Online, September 11, 2000. www.pbs.org/news hour/bb/transportation/july-dec00/mechanics_9-11.html.
43. Traynor, "Aircraft Maintenance."

Chapter Five: Astronauts

44. Quoted in NASA, "So You Want to Be an Astronaut." http://liftoff.msfc.nasa.gov/academy/astronauts/wannabe.html.
45. Quoted in NASA, "So You Want to Be an Astronaut."
46. Official Website of Astronaut Mike Mullane, "Comments on Becoming an Astronaut." www.mikemullane.com/astro.html.
47. Michael E. Long, "Surviving in Space," *National Geographic*, January 2001, p. 11.
48. Quoted in NASA, "How to Become an Astronaut 101." http://space flight.nasa.gov/outreach/jobsinfo/astronaut101.html.
49. Quoted in NASA, "How to Become an Astronaut 101."
50. Quoted in NASA, "OSF Spaceflight Questions and Answers." www.hq.nasa.gov/osf/qanda.html.
51. Quoted in NASA, "An Astronaut's Experiences of the SLS Missions: An Interview with Rhea Seddon." http://lifesci.arc.nasa.gov/lis2/Interviews/Interview_Seddon.html.
52. Quoted in NASA, "An Astronaut's Experiences of the SLS Missions."
53. Quoted in NASA, "OSF Spaceflight Questions and Answers."
54. Quoted in NASA, "How to Become an Astronaut 101."
55. Quoted in NASA, "So You Want to Be an Astronaut."
56. Quoted in NASA, "So You Want to be an Astronaut."
57. Official Website of Astronaut Mike Mullane, "Comments on Becoming an Astronaut."
58. Quoted in NASA, "How to Become an Astronaut 101."

Organizations to Contact

Airline Pilots Association (ALPA)
1625 Massachusetts Ave. NW
Washington, DC 20036
www.alpa.org

ALPA is an advocate for commercial pilot interests, including pay, working conditions, and legal issues. It is the union that represents most commercial airline pilots, and provides career resources and industry news to members and consumers.

Association of Professional Flight Attendants (AFA)
1004 W. Euless Blvd.
Euless, TX 76040
www.afanet.org

AFA, a union that represents the largest proportion of flight attendants in the United States, acts as an advocate of flight attendant interests, including better pay, safety, and working conditions. It also provides industry news related to the profession.

Federal Aviation Administration (FAA)
800 Independence Ave. SW
Washington, DC 20591
www.faa.gov

The FAA provides information on licensing requirements for commercial pilots, aircraft mechanics, and air traffic controllers. It offers a broad spectrum of information related to the aviation industry, and works to promote aviation safety.

National Aeronautics and Space Administration (NASA)
300 E St. SW
Washington, DC 20546-0001
www.nasa.gov

NASA is a federal agency that promotes research and development in space discovery. It offers an immense amount of news and information on astronomy and the latest technology related to space. Information on requirements and applications for the astronaut position are available through NASA, as are interesting biographies on former and current astronauts.

National Air Traffic Controllers Association (NATCA)
1325 Massachusetts Ave. NW
Washington, DC 20005
www.natca.org

NATCA is a union for air traffic controllers and works to promote safety and better working conditions for this profession. It provides information on safety issues, on ATC technology, and on becoming a controller.

Professional Aviation Maintenance Association (PAMA)
636 I St. NW, Suite 300
Washington, DC 20001
www.pama.org

PAMA is a union that promotes the professional treatment and recognition of aircraft mechanics through communication, education, advocacy, and legal support. It also offers information on industry news and technical resources for aircraft mechanics.

For Further Reading

Becky S. Bock and Cheryl A. Cage, *Welcome Aboard! Your Career as a Flight Attendant*. Denver: Cage Consulting, 2000. The authors offer valuable job interviewing tips, explain how the industry works, and profile day-to-day life for flight attendants.

Milovan S. Brenlove, *Vectors to Spare: The Life of an Air Traffic Controller*. Ames: Iowa State University Press, 1993. This autobiography by a fifteen-year veteran air traffic controller sheds light on working with the FAA and what the job is really like.

David Feldman, *How Do Astronauts Scratch an Itch?* New York: Berkeley, 1997. The author answers this question and many others about how astronauts live and work, using interesting facts and theories about life in space.

Ann Graham Gaines, *The Navy in Action (U.S. Military Branches and Careers)*. Berkeley Heights, NJ: Enslow, 2001. This book profiles the history and present-day organization of the U.S. Navy and includes information on career opportunities in this military branch. Additional information is offered about the Naval Academy in Annapolis, Maryland, what boot camp and daily life in the navy are like, and how to join. A special chapter on women and minorities addresses increasing opportunities in the navy.

Tom Kirkwood, *Flight Attendant Job Finder and Career Guide*. River Forest, IL: Planning Communications, 1999. The author provides a wealth of information to help prospective flight attendants decide if the job is right for them and how to break into the industry. Detailed steps for interviewing with airlines, succeeding in training, and profiles of various flight attendants are included. In addition, the author discusses the benefits and downfalls of the job.

Wanda Langley, *The Air Force in Action (U.S. Military Branches and Careers)*. Berkeley Heights, NJ: Enslow, 2001. This interesting guide provides historical and current information on the U.S. Air Force as well as what career opportunities there are for men, women, and minorities. The Air Force Academy is profiled, and the author gives a glimpse of what life is like working for the air force.

Robert P. Mark, *Professional Pilot Career Guide*. New York: McGraw-Hill, 1999. This comprehensive guide offers practical information on where the best career opportunities are for pilots, where and how to learn different types of flying and earn the ratings, and how to succeed in a job interview with an airline, including a list of actual questions commonly asked.

Ceel Pasternak and Linda Thornburg, *Cool Careers for Girls in Air and Space*. Dunedin, FL: Impact, 2001. Ten biographies of women who currently work in the fields of aeronautics and aerospace are presented. Each gives personal motivations for pursuing their particular career, educational training needed, and what everyday life at work is like. Career topics include an astronaut, an air traffic controller, and an airline pilot in addition to several others.

Works Consulted

Books

Captain "X" and Reynolds Dodson, *Unfriendly Skies: Revelations of a Deregulated Airline Pilot.* New York: Doubleday, 1989. The author, who chose to write the book anonymously, is an experienced captain with a major airline. He discusses the effects that deregulation during the 1980s had on the airline industry and gives many personal accounts that illustrate what it's like to learn piloting in the military, flying in bad weather, the hazards of wind phenomena, hijacking, and a perspective on others in the industry, such as air traffic controllers and flight attendants.

The Editors of *Flying Magazine, I Learned About Flying from That!* New York: Delacorte, 1976. This compilation of short articles by pilots spans the 1930s to the 1970s and focuses on the perils encountered in bad weather and from inexperience.

Paul E. Illman, *The Pilot's Air Traffic Control Handbook.* Blue Ridge Summit, PA: Tab Books, 1989. Written by an experienced pilot, this guide offers practical information on using ATC communication to help private pilots fly safer. Chapters include information on the history and development of the FAA and the ATC system, and one chapter focuses on what it takes to be a controller.

Donald S. Lopez, *Aviation (Smithsonian Guides).* New York: Macmillan, 1995. The senior adviser to the director of the National Air and Space Museum recounts the story of how humans attained the ability to fly. Twentieth-century changes are chronicled through both world wars and the dawn of commercial jetliners to current technological advances in aircraft.

John Thorn, ed., *The Armchair Aviator.* New York: Charles Scribner's Sons, 1983. This anthology of articles about flying covers everything from humankind's first attempts hundreds of years ago to twentieth-century flight. Articles and sketches cover topics such as military flying, commercial flying, the meaning of aviation, test piloting, and more.

Periodicals

Francis X. Donnelly, "Mechanics Want Pay Like Lives Depend on It," *Detroit News,* April 6, 2001.

Chip Jones, "The Plane Truth: Inside the Hangar with Aircraft Mechanics at Richmond International Airport," *Richmond Times-Dispatch,* August 6, 2001.

Michael E. Long, "Surviving in Space," *National Geographic*, January 2001.

Mozart A. T. Pastrano, "Terror at 6,000 Feet," *Philippine Daily Inquirer*, January 14, 2001.

Internet Sources
Aviation News Web, "Flight Attendant Reports." www.aviationnewsweb. com/aviation1/flight_attendant_reports.htm.

Joel Freeman, "How Becoming an Airline Pilot Works," How Stuff Works. www.howstuffworks.com/pilot.htm.

Darcy Frey, "Something's Got to Give." *New York Times*, March 24, 1996. www.airtrafficcafe.com/something_got_to_give.shtml.

Kelli Gant, "Women in Aviation," Ninety-Nines. www.ninety-nines. org/wia.html.

KiwiCareers Website, "Avionics Engineering Tradesperson." www.careers. co.nz/jobs/4c_mec/j38363h.htm.

NASA, "An Astronaut's Experiences of the SLS Missions: An Interview with Rhea Seddon." http://lifesci.arc.nasa.gov/lis2/Interviews/ Interview_Seddon.html.

———, "How to Become an Astronaut 101." http://spaceflight.nasa.gov/ outreach/jobsinfo/astronaut101.html.

———, "OSF Spaceflight Questions and Answers." www.hq.nasa. gov/osf/qanda.html.

———, "So You Want to Be an Astronaut." http://liftoff.msfc.nasa.gov/ academy/astronauts/wannabe.html.

Bill O'Brien, "Grease Monkey," Aircraft Maintenance. www.qtm.net/ ~jetdoc/amt.htm.

Harold L. O'Brien, "Interview—Avionics and Instrumentation, Harold L. O'Brien." http://wings.avkids.com/Careers/obrien.html.

Official Website of Astronaut Mike Mullane, "Comments on Becoming an Astronaut." www.mikemullane.com/astro.html.

Ted Robbins, "Wanted: Mechanics," NewsHour with Jim Lehrer Online, September 11, 2000. www.pbs.org/newshour/bb/transportation/ july-dec00/mechanics_9-11.html.

Wendy Stafford, "The Mystique of the Flight Attendant," Aviation Career.net, August 20, 2001. www.aviationcareer.net/features/fa_0411 2001_03.cfm.

Travel, "The Passenger from Hell," August 17, 1999. www.salon.com/ travel/diary/hest/1999/08/17/passenger/html.

Adam Traynor, "Aircraft Maintenance," Jet Careers Website. www.jet careers.com/maintenance.htm.

World Wide Aviation Employment Assistance Website, "A Flight Attendant Talks About Her Job." www.avjobs.com/careers/flightattendant/ flightattendanttalks.htm.

Index

future career potential for, 80
job risks of, 77–80
living in space and, 74–75
management opportunities
and, 77
medical care in space and, 79
preparation for mission and,
71–72
reentry and, 75–76
research and, 70–71, 73–74,
77
rewards of job of, 80
salaries of, 77
screening process for, 65–67
Spacelab and, 70
space shuttle and, 72, 73
space suits and, 69, 70
specializing and, 70
training for, 67, 69–70
work schedules of, 77–78
Astronaut Selection Board,
66–67
avionics technicians, 56–57

Bernoulli effect, 19
black box, 55

Cape Canaveral, 72
cargo planes, 15
cockpit, 16, 61
commercial pilot's license, 13
Concorde, 15
control tower, 39
copilot, 19
courier airlines, 14

Edwards Air Force Base, 76
en route control centers, 48–51
en route controllers, 48–51

see also air traffic controllers

FAA. *See* Federal Aviation
Administration
FAA Academy, 47
Federal Aviation
Administration (FAA)
aircraft mechanic licensing
and, 57–59
equipment modernization and,
44
flight schools, 14
future air traffic control system
development, 44
history of, 41
pilots' examinations and
licensing and, 12
responsibilities of, 41
space program and, 41
first officer, 19, 24–25
flight, 19
flight attendants
abilities required of, 26, 28, 31
advancement in job and,
35–36
basic function of, 26
duties of, 26, 28–31
educational requirements for,
34
future job stability for, 37
health risks of, 31–32
hijacking and, 29, 36
history of, 33
"reserve" and, 35–36
salaries of, 37
screening process for employment as, 34
seniority and, 34, 36, 37
stress and, 31–32

Picture Credits

Cover: Image Bank/Getty

© AFP/CORBIS: 18

Bruce Daniels: 59

© Carl & Ann Purcell/CORBIS: 62

© Charles E. Rotkin/CORBIS: 40

© CORBIS: 21, 69, 78

© Dave Bartruff/CORBIS: 57

© George Hall/CORBIS: 50, 54

© Hulton/Archive: 10, 33

© Hulton-Deutsch Collection/CORBIS: 49

© Jacques M. Chenet/CORBIS: 27

© Lawrence Manning/CORBIS: 46

© Military Picture Library/CORBIS: 13

© NASA/Roger Ressmeyer/CORBIS: 66, 71, 75, 76

National Archives: 9 (both)

© Owen Franklin/CORBIS: 30

© Patrick Bennett/CORBIS: 53

© Randy Wells/CORBIS: 43

© Roger Ressmeyer/CORBIS: 17, 35, 37

© Ron Watts/CORBIS: 39

© Tim Wright/CORBIS: 48, 63

United States Department of Agriculture: 22

© Vince Streano/CORBIS: 11

About the Author

Christina M. Girod received her undergraduate degree from the University of California at Santa Barbara. She worked with speech- and language-impaired students and taught elementary school for six years in Denver, Colorado. She has written feature articles, short biographies, and organizational and country profiles for educational multimedia materials. The topics she has covered include politicians, humanitarians, environmentalists, entertainers, and geography. She has also written several titles for Lucent Books on subjects such as Native Americans, entertainers, and disabilities. Her most recent books are *Connecticut*, *South Carolina*, and *Georgia*, part of the Thirteen Colonies series. Girod lives in Santa Maria, California, with her husband, Jon Pierre, and daughter, Joni.